ALLY BLAKE

Billionaire on Her Doorstep

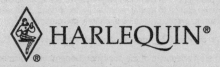

HARLEQUIN®

TORONTO • NEW YORK • LONDON
AMSTERDAM • PARIS • SYDNEY • HAMBURG
STOCKHOLM • ATHENS • TOKYO • MILAN • MADRID
PRAGUE • WARSAW • BUDAPEST • AUCKLAND

ISBN-13: 978-0-373-03959-3
ISBN-10:   0-373-03959-X

BILLIONAIRE ON HER DOORSTEP

First North American Publication 2007.

Tom gave in first. He took two bold steps to stand before her, toe-to-toe. He looked down into her eyes—eyes she knew were wide with disbelief and desire. He lifted a gentle hand, resting the backs of his knuckles against her cheek, and suddenly she couldn't remember how to breathe.

More to keep her balance than out of any form of invitation, Maggie lifted a hand to rest against his chest. She felt a tremble shudder through Tom's rock-solid body, and only then did she finally recognise the depth of the attraction that had been simmering between them for days.

It had crept up on her, lacing surreptitiously through the back recesses of her mind until the feeling was woven so tight she had the horrible sense she would never be able to fully unravel it.

She'd counted on herself being more careful. More resilient. More uncompromising. After what she'd been through in the past couple of years, that should have been a given. What she hadn't counted on was Tom Campbell walking through her door....

Harlequin Romance®

**brings you a fresh new story
from Australian author**

Ally Blake

**Curl up and indulge yourself
with this contemporary, vibrant and
heartwarming novel.**

Praise for Ally Blake...

Having once been a professional cheerleader, **Ally Blake**'s motto is "Smile and the world smiles with you." One way to make Ally smile is by sending her away on holidays, especially to locations that inspire her writing. New York and Italy are by far her favorite destinations. Other things that make her smile are the gracious city of Melbourne, the gritty Collingwood football team and her gorgeous husband, Mark.

Reading romance novels was a smile-worthy pursuit from long back. So, with such valuable preparation already behind her, she wrote and sold her first book. Her career as a writer also gives her a perfectly reasonable excuse to indulge in her stationery addiction. That alone is enough to keep her grinning every day!

Ally would love you to visit her at her Web site www.allyblake.com.

Look out for Ally's next sparkling story
Millionaire to the Rescue
out in October, only from Harlequin Romance®

To my gorgeous husband, Mark,
and our fabulous first ten years together.

Love you always....

CHAPTER ONE

TOM CAMPBELL slammed the door of his trusty rusty Ute, not bothering to lock it. Not because he wouldn't have cared if it was pinched. Or because the area had an unparalleled neighbourhood watch programme. But because it didn't need to.

The good people of Portsea were more likely to make a steal as doctors or lawyers or footballers than to steal a dilapidated tradesman's car. For Portsea was the land of high brushwood fences and vast homes with purely ornamental tennis courts and architecturally designed swimming pools posturing magnificently on the tip of the Mornington Peninsula.

Tom hitched his tool belt higher on his hips, threw a pink pillowcase full of old rags over his shoulder and strode through one such brushwood gate graced with the word 'Belvedere' burnt into a lump of moss-covered wood.

From the top of the dipping dirt driveway he caught glimpses of white wood and a slate-grey tiled roof, which was not an unusual combination for a house by the beach. What was unusual was that, unlike other properties in Portsea, Belvedere wasn't manicured to within an inch of its life. In fact it wasn't manicured at all.

As the foliage cleared, he saw a house that looked as if it had been built over fifty years by half a dozen architects with incompatible visions. At least five levels ambled down the sloping hill towards the cliff's edge. Most of the original pale green shutters were closed to the morning light and by the deep orange rust on their hinges he guessed many hadn't been opened in months. The rest was hidden behind what looked to be years of neglected foliage. If the local council had any idea that this place was in such disrepair they'd be up here in a Sorrento second waving their ordinances on beautification and escalating land value.

Many of the homes in Portsea were empty most of the year and needed nothing more than basic upkeep by overpaid full-time gardeners. As a hire-a-handyman he only did odd jobs. But this place... Already he could see it could do with a lick of paint. And the garden could do with some tender love and care, or a backhoe. It was a renovator's dream. And Tom would be sure to tell Lady Bryce all of that once he had a damn clue what he was doing there in the first place.

Tom smiled to himself. *Lady* Bryce. That was what the Barclay sisters, the doyennes of Portsea who ran the local haberdashery, had labelled her because she hadn't yet deigned to frequent their fine establishment.

He'd never met her either, though he had spied her driving down the Sorrento main street in her big black Jeep, large sunglasses and ponytail, eyes ahead, mouth in a determined straight line and fingers clamped to the steering wheel as though for dear life. And when weighing up working for a woman who at first glance seemed pretty highly strung against the time it would take away from his fishing he had considered declining politely. But, as usual, when it came to the crunch, he hadn't had it in him to say no.

He could picture his cousin Alex laughing at him even *con-*

sidering turning down a damsel in distress, for Alex seemed to think Tom had some sort of knight in shining armour complex. Tom thought Alex ought to mind his own business.

He ducked out of the way of a low-hanging vine, watched his step for fear of turning an ankle and slowed as a magnificent ten-foot-high wood-carved double front door loomed amidst a shower of hanging ferns. The right door was ajar, but guarded by a sizeable old red-brown hound with a great big smiley-face charm with the word 'Smiley' written upon it hanging off his thick collar. .

'Smiley, hey?' Tom said.

The dog lifted its weary head and blinked at him, its floppy ears and sad expression not changing a lick to show that he felt any pleasure at the unexpected company.

Tom reached down and gave the poor old soul a rub on the head. 'Is the lady of the house about?'

A sudden crashing noise followed by a seriously *un*ladylike spray of words told Tom that the lady of the house certainly was about.

'Hello,' he called out, but he was met with silence as sudden as the previous verbal spray had been. Not finding any evidence of a doorbell, he stepped over the melancholic guard dog and walked further inside the entrance to find himself face to face with a square stain on the wall, evidence that once upon a time a picture had hung there, a garden bench that had a mildewed look about it as though it had been relegated from outside, covered in a pile of unopened mail, and yet another fern living its sad, bedraggled life in a bright new ceramic pot.

Another curse word, this one softer than the last, caught his hearing and he followed it like a beacon to find himself in a huge main room with sweeping wooden floors in need of a good polish, lit bright by a series of uncurtained ceiling-to-floor French windows through which he had a thicket-shrouded view of the sun glinting off glorious Port Phillip Bay.

Images piled up in his mind of what he could do with this place if given half a chance. And the whole summer, and an open cheque book, and his old team at his side, and a time machine to take him back ten years… He shook his head to clear away the wool-gathering within.

The room he was in was empty. No furniture. No pictures on the walls. Nothing. Well, nothing bar a twisting cream telephone cord snaking across the middle of the room to the far wall, where a large grey drop cloth, buckets of paint, several flat, square structures draped in fabric, a rickety old table, which held numerous jars of coloured water and different sized paintbrushes, and an easel with a three-by-four-foot canvas slathered in various shades of blue.

And, in front of it all, wearing no shoes, paint-spattered jeans, a T-shirt that might at one time have been white and a navy bandanna covering most of her biscuit-blonde hair was the lady in question.

Tom cleared his throat and called out, 'Ms Bryce?'

She spun on her heel with such speed that paint from her brush splattered across the all-blue canvas.

Tom winced. It was red paint.

'Holy heck!' she blurted in a toned down version of the language from earlier. Her voice was husky, her high cheekbones pink and her pale grey eyes aglow.

Well, what do you know? Tom thought. *My lucky day.* For Lady Bryce was a knockout. He wished his cousin Alex was there with him now so he could poke him hard in the side and tell him—*this* is why you never say no to a damsel in distress.

'Who the hell are you?' the lady asked, seemingly not nearly as impressed with him. But the day was young. 'And what are you doing in my house?'

Tom actually thought it pretty obvious who he was considering the family of tools swinging low on his hips. But the lady looked as if she knew how to wield that paintbrush of hers as a lethal weapon so he answered her query.

'I'm Tom Campbell, your friendly neighbourhood handyman,' he said, deciding to pull out all the stops in the hopes she wouldn't use that thing as a javelin. He smiled the smile that had got him out of trouble on any number of occasions and opened his arms wide to show he was not a threat in any way, shape or form. 'You called a few days ago, asking if I could come around today to fix…something.'

The lady blinked. Several times in quick succession. Long eyelashes swooping against her flushed cheeks. Unfairly long eyelashes, he thought, especially for a woman who continued to send off such fierce keep-away vibes. Then her eyes scooted down to rest on his tools.

Tom clenched his toes in his boots to stop himself from shuffling under her acute gaze.

'Right,' she said suddenly, punctuating the sharp word by pointing her skinny paintbrush his way.

And dammit if he didn't actually flinch!

Tom took a slow, deep breath. He'd let those crazy old Barclay sisters get inside his head so much that he'd actually begun to believe this poor woman could be some kind of nut job, simply because she hadn't found the need for haberdashery, whatever haberdashery might be.

So far nothing worse had happened than red splatters on her picture. So far she seemed merely antisocial at worst. And at best? Unimpressed by him in particular. Lucky him.

'Tom Campbell. The handyman,' she repeated. 'Okay.' She unconsciously twirled the offensive paintbrush in her fingers like a cheerleader's baton before turning back to her work-table, choosing a water pot at random and swooshing the brush in the dirty liquid.

She glanced briefly at her big blue painting, saw the red splatters and swore again. It seemed she wasn't the type to pull her punches because she had company.

Tom felt his cheeks tugging into a smile. If the Barclay sisters knew her penchant for *French* he was quite sure they would drop the 'Lady' moniker quick smart.

With a shake of her head, she tiptoed off the drop cloth, scrunching her toes as she wiped her bare feet at the edge, and moved to join him.

She walked with a sort of natural elegance, like a ballet dancer, heel to toe, long legs fluid. Her skin had an almost translucent appearance and her clothes hung off her as if she had lost weight quickly and had not found the time or inclination to put it back on.

She was pretty tall too. She must have been near five-ten. Tom drew himself up to his full six feet and one half inch to compensate. And though her eyes were grey, when she wasn't glaring at him they held hints of the same pale blue found in the clear spring sky behind her.

She pulled the navy bandanna from her hair and used it to wipe her hands, then tucked it into the back pocket of her jeans. Next she yanked a hair-band from her ponytail and shook the straight length loose until it hung long and dishevelled halfway down her back, before gathering it all and folding it into a messy low bun.

This little act was merely a habit, he was sure. Her move-ments were fast, spare and not meant to impress. But they impressed him. In fact he found the whole hair shaking move pretty darned satisfying.

Or maybe *that* was the point after all. Maybe that was how she got her kicks—conning local workmen into her web for a quickie before tumbling them off the cliff on to the jagged rocks behind her secluded home. Perhaps her infrequent trips into town at the wheel of her suburban tank were to buy quick-lime and shovels.

She strode past him and into the massive kitchen and, despite his lively imaginings, Tom followed. There were no scrawled pictures on the fridge. No post-its or shopping lists. No flowers on the window ledge. No jars full of mismatched utensils as were to be found in most of the homes he worked in. According to the Barclay sisters, she'd lived here for months, but the place looked as if she'd just moved in and hadn't unpacked all her boxes.

Still, though he had as much fun seeing inside other people's homes as the next guy, if she didn't have a job for him in the next ten seconds he was going to walk. It really was a glorious day outside and the fish would no doubt be biting…

'What would you like me to do for you, Ms Bryce?'

She switched on the kettle, then turned and leaned her backside against the sink and stared him down, her grey eyes shrewd, distant and enormous.

'Maggie,' she said. 'Firstly I would like you to call me Maggie.'

He nodded. 'Only if you call me Tom.' Having been brought up to believe that a proper introduction required it, Tom reached out to shake hands.

Maggie reached forward herself and gave his hand a brisk pump. Her palm was neither soft nor smooth. Her lean hand rasped against his, her calloused palm creating a strange sensation against his own work-roughened mitt.

Nevertheless, he kept a hold a moment longer than he really ought. As he soon found himself caught in a wave of her perfume.

For, of all the scents to choose from in the big wide world, she wore dark and delicious Sonia Rykiel. He was sure of it. One Christmas a cute blonde at the perfume counter of a department store in Sydney had convinced him to buy it for his sister. But, considering Tess had been bright and vivacious, with not a lick of the dark and delicious about her personality, it had been a running joke between them that she'd never worn the stuff. But on Maggie Bryce he could have sworn the balmy scent wasn't worn so much as radiating from her pores.

Despite the thorns, and the colourful vocabulary, and the bohemian lack of furniture, she was seriously lovely. And he was definitely loveable. As far as he saw it, they were a summer romance just waiting to happen. All he had to do was convince her.

'So you're living all the way out here alone?' he asked, gradually letting her go.

'I have Smiley,' she said, reclaiming her hand and crossing her arms. 'You no doubt met him at the front door.'

'He's an interesting variety of male companionship,' he said. 'I'll give him that.'

She snorted elegantly, though Tom'd never known it possible to do so. Then, looking him dead in the eye, she said, 'I'll take Smiley over the rest any day.'

'Sure,' he said. 'Who wouldn't?'

Okay, so there must have been any number of women who thought him not their type; during his past life in Sydney when he'd at one time been seen as the catch of the town, and again since moving to Sorrento where he was now regarded as contentedly uncatchable. But at least he'd never had one look him the eye and as much as said, *Don't even think about it.* Until now.

'Smiley obviously can't wield a set of tools with any sort of finesse or I am beginning to believe you would never have called me for help,' he said.

'And Smiley has already had a good talking to about that, I assure you.'

Now that he knew how, Tom snorted elegantly himself, despite his bruised pride. For beneath the cool demeanour this one was spunky. And Tom liked nothing if not a spunky woman.

The kettle boiled and she blithely ignored him while she set to making coffee for them both.

Perhaps it wasn't *him per se*; perhaps she wasn't into blue-collar men. Women living on their own in Portsea clearly fell into two categories: those who looked straight through men dressed like him and those who saw him as the perfect antidote to whatever white-collar dullard had made them rich and single in the first place.

If that was her problem, he could always accidentally drop an ATM statement on her floor so that she could see he wasn't quite the unfortunate he seemed to be. Maybe that would perk her up a bit. Clear that furrowed brow. Create a cheeky sparkle in those impassive grey eyes.

Unless of course she wasn't his type either. Now that he thought about it, she was pretty tall, and he liked putting his arm around a woman's shoulders without pulling a muscle. Too blunt, where he'd rather have charming subtlety. Too cool, where he preferred everything in his life to be warm—his days, his nights, the woman in his arms during his days and nights. Yep, it was probably for the best if he just left the lady well enough alone.

'Are you available for longer jobs?' she asked.

She passed him a hot black coffee and pressed the sugar shaker an inch his way, then looked at him beneath her long lashes as she pursed her lips and blew across the top of her own mug.

'I'm on call for a number of businesses around. Okay, on call might be putting it a little too formally. *In the phone book* is more factual. Though the Barclay sisters will brook no excuses if they need a light bulb changed.'

Maggie swished a hand across her face as though flapping away a particularly unimportant fly. 'It's not that big a job, I'm sure,' she said.

Tom begged to differ. Belvedere was a colossal job waiting to happen. The ceiling of the kitchen could do with being lifted another two feet at least. Add a skylight and it would feel twice as big. Tear away the thick, dusty concave mouldings and he'd put money on the fact that the original cornices would be revealed beneath. 'What sort of job?' he asked.

'I can't get down to the beach,' Maggie said, cutting his flight of fancy off at the knees.

'The beach?'

'The backyard is utterly overgrown,' she continued. 'Brambles, vines and brush so thick and so tall and so broad you can't see beyond.'

'Brambles,' he repeated. Thick, intertwined, thorny, scratchy brambles. Excellent.

'Right. Brambles. Remember that really hot day last week, so still there was not a sea breeze to speak of?'

Tom nodded. He remembered feeling as if spring was near its end. Soon the tourists would swarm the place, his phone would ring off the hook and he and his little boat wouldn't have any time alone for a good three months.

'I had it in mind that day to find out what sort of private

beach this place might have,' Maggie said, 'and I discovered there was no way through without a chainsaw or a pole vault. You may have noticed that I am living here with the bare basics, thus I had neither instrument handy.'

Attractive, spunky and a self-deprecating sense of humour to boot? Tom leant his hip against the bench and cocked his left foot against the cupboard door, wondering if he had been too hasty in deciding she was too tall for him. Besides which, Portsea and next door Sorrento in which he lived were small and mostly transient communities, so it would be sensible to get to know her better. In case he one day needed to borrow a cup of sugar.

'Right. A beach, you say. So how long have you lived here now?' he asked.

'I moved here from Melbourne about six months ago. Give or take,' she said.

Well, now, that wasn't so hard for her, was it? That was decidedly social. Tom made a move to ask a follow-up question but she got there first.

'Shall we?' she asked, pushing away from the bench.

Right. *Now* she was in a hurry.

Maggie led him out the back door, which was held open by a massive red earthenware pot, on to the shady veranda which ran the length of the back of the house and down a set of rickety wooden steps that opened up to a small paved courtyard as heavy with weeds as the front walk.

And beyond that? A thirty metre wide wall of thick, sharp, decade-old scrub, as tall as two men. Tom couldn't even tell how deep he might have to dig before he hit the cliff face, or where any path or steps down to the beach might even begin. If there in fact was a beach there at all.

'Nice ferns,' he said to stop himself from saying the rest,

as he had to duck under another row of bedraggled plants in hanging pots.

'They came with the house,' she said. 'You may have noticed I'm not much of a gardener.'

Noticed? He'd become pretty darned intimate with a whole range of plants on his way in. He was certain he would be finding leaves and twigs in numerous nooks and crannies when he stripped for his shower later that night.

'I noticed,' was all he said, especially since Maggie had now decided to be friendly. He had to think of the future possibility of sugar after all.

'I'm resigned to the fact that I have a black thumb,' she said. She held her right thumb up between them and it told a different story, covered as it was in blue paint. 'Okay, so it's in fact a blue thumb. What does that mean?'

'Perhaps you are doomed to breed depressed plants rather than dead ones.'

And at that, for the first time since he'd laid eyes on her, Maggie smiled. Her eyes gleamed, her cheeks bloomed into rosy mounds and she even showed a hint of neat white teeth with the tiniest of overbites. The fact that Tom had always had a thing for overbites was not lost on him.

'I think you might be right,' she said, the overbite sadly disappearing as she brought her features back under strict control. She flicked another glance at his tool belt. 'You can do gardens, I hope?'

'I can. And I have. I am a verified genius at mowing and pulling weeds. I've even fixed my fair share of cracked pool pavers.' He took another step towards the seemingly impenetrable wall of green and fingered a sharp-edged leaf. 'But now's my chance to fulfil the lifelong dream to use a scythe.'

He glanced sideways in time to see Maggie's gaze flicker

to his. A small muscle moved in her cheek and he thought himself about to be on the receiving end of another smile. Another vision of her two front teeth tucking over her terribly attractive full bottom lip. But he was mistaken.

'I'm glad to oblige,' she said with a small shrug of her slight shoulders. 'It's not often a person gets to be involved in the culmination of another's lifelong dream.'

Tom grinned and Maggie frowned.

'So, how long do you think it will take?' she asked.

'I'll have more of an idea by the end of the day,' he said.

'Right. Then I shall leave you to it,' she said. 'There's some sort of shed around the side of the house. Feel free to see if there is anything in there you can use. No scythe, though, I'm afraid.'

'No scythe *and* no pole vault? How do you survive out here?' Tom asked, smiling himself, showing her how it was done, seeing if he could again encourage hers out to play, but all he got for his trouble was a cool grey stare.

'Tremendous amounts of coffee seem to do the trick,' she said, deadpan. She blinked at him once more, those long curling lashes making themselves known deep down in his gut.

He was absolutely certain she was deciding whether she really wanted the likes of him hanging around her place.

Her frown lines diminished and he determined she had made the decision that she did. Want him. Around the place.

Then, without a further word, Maggie Bryce took her long legs, cool eyes and adorable overlapping teeth back upstairs, leaving Tom, his tools and his overactive imagination to their own devices.

CHAPTER TWO

A FEW hours later, Maggie glanced down at the mug of Jamaican Roast perched in between her water jars to find it had become paint dust swimming in cold dregs.

She moved to the edge of her drop cloth, wiped her feet—which was more a decade-old habit than any intention to keep the floor paint-free—refixed her hair and then shuffled into the kitchen to make another coffee.

As she waited for the kettle to boil, she leant her backside against the kitchen bench and stretched the crick in her neck. The tendon along the top of her right shoulder was aching. Back in Melbourne she would have taken a quick trip to Maurice for a life-affirming massage. But back in Melbourne she had been able to afford Maurice. Here, with her single bank account dwindling to near drastic levels while she paid the colossal mortgage on the big house around her, she had to make do with a heat pack at the end of the day.

She started at the anomalous sound of thrashing foliage breaching the unvarying Portsea peace and quiet. At first she thought it was Smiley out adventuring. Then she remembered the stranger in her midst. She turned and, standing on tiptoe, looked through the kitchen window. But he must have moved somewhere under the house.

When she'd found Tom Campbell's name in the phone book she'd half expected some wizened, semi-retired jack-of-all-trades working to earn extra bingo money. She'd *fully* expected wizened old Tom Campbell to take one look at her brambles, run a sorry arm across his wrinkled forehead and claim the way through an impossibility.

She'd been prepared for that eventuality, ready for it to be the last in a long line of signs that her experimental life at the beach had come to an end. The other clear signs being no money left in the bank, no brilliance happening on the canvas and not even the slightest sense that she would ever fit in, no matter how hard she wished she could.

What she hadn't been prepared for was Tom Campbell himself. He'd surprised the heck out of her by actually being there when he said he would, and also by being the complete opposite of wizened. He was in his mid-thirties with dark hair in need of a cut. He was broad, strapping, in shockingly good health. And had the kind of smile built to warm the coldest heart. Then he'd further compounded her surprise by taking one look at her impossible brambles and saying, 'Can do'.

The sight of that thirty metre wide wall of thorns should have sent him running in terror. The guy must have needed a pay cheque worse than she did.

She bit at her bottom lip, not all that sure if she was relieved or disappointed that his *can do* attitude had given her decision time a stay of execution. She *was* sure it would cost a considerable amount to pull apart the great twisted wall of leaves and branches blocking her from the promise of—what? A few jagged rocks? Maybe, if she was lucky, a skinny patch of sand? But if he could get through the wall to the virgin beach beyond, then she could stretch out her finances and her resolve until then.

The kettle boiled and, with a fresh mug warming her tender, wood-scratched palms, Maggie slipped out of the kitchen and through the back door. She eased over to the edge of the balcony, rested her forearms along the brittle railing and looked one floor below to where her handyman was once again hard at work.

At some stage that morning he had ditched his sweater. His soft grey T-shirt, now drenched in sweat, twisted around his torso as he used his substantial might to heave threads of dead vines from the mass of brush. His tool belt lay neatly across the bottom step next to a lumpy pillowcase with a rag poking out the top.

Maggie's cheek twitched as she leant her chin on her palm and thought there was something to be said about the confidence of a man who took a pink pillowcase to a worksite.

Smiley ambled up behind her and nuzzled against her hand. 'Hey, buddy, how's it hangin'?' she asked.

Smiley looked up at her in bemusement.

'Now I know it's not often that your big city guard dog instincts have had to come into play down here, but how about next time you warn me when we have a stranger at the front door? Deal?'

Smiley slumped to the floor on top of her feet and Maggie knew that was all the answer she was going to get.

The scent of the Jamaican Roast tickled her nose and with an enthusiast's satisfied sigh she took a long leisurely sip, relishing the feeling of the hot liquid scorching her tongue and throat. Her stomach thanked her. But it needed more.

She glanced again over the railing. It would take some time, days even, to clear the wilderness choking her backyard, even once he had a chainsaw. And though the guy was an accomplished flirt, and she had no intention of flirting back, that didn't mean she oughtn't to be civil.

She would bring him lunch. Nothing flash. A plain cheese and tomato sandwich would surely show she wasn't interested in anything he had to offer besides his skilful hands. Which were only welcome in her garden. On her plants.

'Inside,' she said to Smiley. 'I must be more famished than I realise.'

Ten minutes later, Maggie walked down her wooden back steps with the first meal she had made for someone other than herself or Smiley in nigh on six months. Even Freya, Sandra and Ashleigh brought their own food when they came over for their regular play date each Wednesday. And sensibly so. Cheese and tomato on white was about as gastronomically adventurous as Maggie could be.

Tom turned at the sound of creaking steps. There were tracks in his dark hair where his fingers had pushed his too long fringe out of his eyes.

'I figured you might be hungry,' Maggie said.

'Starving,' he said. 'Thanks.' He breathed in deep and stood taller, stretching his arms over his head, arms jam-packed with sinewy muscles.

Maggie cleared her throat and turned away to put his sandwich and cup of black coffee on the step above his tool belt. She was all prepared to shoot a farewell wave and jog back up the stairs when she noticed a trail of dirt smeared across his shiny forehead. She seriously considered leaving him with a smudge on his face for the rest of the day. But his spoiled aesthetic was too much of a shame for her artist's eye to leave be.

'You've got a smear,' she mumbled, waving a hand in his general direction. 'Right across your forehead. Dirt. Grass. General mess.'

He shrugged, his hands dropping to hang casually at his

sides. 'It won't be the last of the day. This is the kind of job that leaves its mark on a man. As is yours, I see.'

He glanced downward and Maggie did the same to find her bare feet covered in splotches of blue paint with a dash of that blasted red thrown in for good measure. She wiggled her toes back up at herself. Toes that had once been pedicured on a weekly basis now had nails so short they looked like the feet of a rambunctious teenager.

'Occupational hazard,' she said, tucking the filthier of her feet behind the other.

'Not such a bad one—getting dirty,' he said. 'At least we don't have to worry about things like hypertension and stress like they do up in the city.' He smiled at her, as though awaiting a response.

Maggie blinked at him. He wanted to chat?

She reminded herself that she had a very much unfinished painting upstairs awaiting her return. But then again it would be rude to just cut and run…

'High blood pressure they can keep,' she said. 'But I do miss the stress of living in the city.'

'Why's that?' he asked.

'Without a strict deadline to keep me focused, I give in to distraction all too easily. I have been known to take navel gazing to the heights of an art form.'

Tom's dark hazel eyes skittered down her front to land upon the general region of the navel in question.

To distract herself from the ridiculous need to tug at her T-shirt, she blurted, 'And I *desperately* miss the traffic noise at night. The steady whoosh below my apartment window. I still haven't found a way to fall asleep before two in the morning without it. My friend Freya seems to think I should thank my lucky stars that I've replaced car fumes for sea air.

But I'm not sure it's natural for a coffee-drinking, night owl workaholic to transform into a late-sleeping, star-gazing, shell-collecting yoga zealot overnight.'

When she stopped to take a breath Maggie realised she had gone a mile further into her personal zone than she had ever meant to go. But, rather than looking at her as if she was some kind of chump in need of therapy, as Freya did when she said such things, Tom nodded.

'I was like that for the first few weeks after I moved here from Sydney.'

'*You're* from Sydney?' When his right eyebrow disappeared beneath his fringe, she pressed her lips together and tilted her nose a little higher in the air.

Tom gave a small bow. 'Born and bred. A long time ago in a galaxy far, far away. Though I've been here for a while now, so the sand and salt has permeated my skin for good. Give it time.' His eyes crinkled kindly. 'You'll get there too.'

Maggie's cheeks warmed. Was it that obvious that salt and sand had yet to make it on to *her* all-time top one hundred list of favourite things? And was it that obvious that she wished more than anything in the world that they had? For it would mean that she really could change the patterns of her life?

'Were you in the same line of work in Sydney?' she asked, deliberately changing the subject.

Tom paused, but only briefly. 'In a manner of speaking. I worked in restorations.'

'Of houses?'

'Some,' he said. 'At first. Then we expanded and eventually concentrated on the restorations of heritage listed buildings.'

'Lots of those in Sydney,' she said. 'Not so many here. So why did you move?' Okay, so now *she* was asking a heck of a lot of questions. But that 'you'll get there' comment had stuck in her craw. And, like a dog with a bone she couldn't leave it be.

'We used to spend our summers here when we were kids, and my cousin Alex still lives down the road in Rye,' he said.

'So far as I can tell, people around here would rather knock an old place down than renovate,' she said. 'Belvedere might well have gone that way if I hadn't bought her when I did. So there can't be much call for restoration guys.'

'Doesn't matter,' he said. 'I don't do that sort of thing any more.'

'Why not?'

He paused again and she noticed that he was no longer smiling all that much. But by then it was too late.

'I changed a lot—' he said '—my trade, my location, my lifestyle, right after my little sister, Tess, died.'

Maggie's solar plexus seized up and a small 'Oh,' escaped her lips. Suddenly she wished she could take it all back—the conversation, the sandwich, the phone call asking him to come out and clear her brambles.

She waved a hand in front of her face until he became lost within the fast shifting movement of her open fingers. 'Tom, I'm sorry, it's none of my business. I—'

'It's okay,' he said, shrugging, but even after knowing him for all of five minutes she could see that his inner light had dimmed. 'The funny thing is, if she was here now in my stead she would have bent your ear until it hurt. Although she had the same skill with a paintbrush as you have with plants, she adored all things art. Funny, funny girl… At any rate, when she died it was an easy decision to come here, even though the call for restorations wasn't all that significant.'

Maggie had no idea what to say. Knowing more about the guy than she had ever meant to unearth, she shot him a tight-lipped smile, flattened her heel against the first step and made a move to retreat before things became any more uncomfortable, when he said, 'You want my advice for a good night's sleep?'

Her foot stopped moving. 'If you think it'll help.'

'You just have to give yourself over to the sounds of the ocean—the seagulls, the waves hitting the shore, the distant horns as ships pass one another in the night. And, when you do, you'll wonder why you haven't been a beachcomber all your life.'

His smile came creeping back, brightening his dark eyes and adding oodles of character to his too handsome face. Sceptical, about a good many things, Maggie shook her head. 'It can't be that easy.'

'You know people actually buy CDs of ocean waves to help them sleep?' Tom asked.

'Best of luck to them,' she said.

At her determined mulishness Tom laughed. Maggie wasn't all that surprised that he had a natural, throaty, infectious laugh. For she was coming to see that he was living proof that the Wednesday girls were right. If Tom was any indication, maybe this place, with its peace and quiet and fresh air and sunshine, really did hold the elixir for a long and happy life.

A drop of sweat ran down Tom's face. His arm came up, blocking her view and wiping the drop away. But when his hand dropped she found herself looking into a pair of smiling hazel eyes, filled with unambiguous invitation.

Maggie swallowed. Hard. But she couldn't look away.

Then Tom took a sudden step towards her.

It was so unexpected that Maggie flinched, and abruptly, so that the back of her heel whacked against the edge of the step, making a horrid crunching sound that seemed to reverberate in the sudden deep well of silence.

The poor guy withdrew, hands raised in the international sign of surrender. 'I was just going for the sandwich, I promise,' he said.

Maggie would have kicked herself if only her heel wasn't already so sore. Instead she dug her fingernails into her palms as she willed her body to rock back on to flat feet.

'I know. Of course. I'm— Sorry, I was startled because I was away with the fairies. Another occupational hazard.' She stepped aside, leaving the way between the man and his food clear.

He moved, more slowly this time, picked up his meal and backed away as though he knew instinctively just how much space she needed in order to breathe. He bit off a quarter of the sandwich in one go. Then, after washing it down with a healthy slug of coffee, he leaned against the canted railing, shook his boyish fringe from his eyes and breathed out what sounded to Maggie like a sigh of contentment.

Envy of his every laid-back action arced around her as she tried to remember how long it had been since she'd done anything in *contentment*. The pile of half-finished canvases stacked against the wall in her great room reminded her that it had been months and months. Even since long before she had arrived in Portsea.

And then on that stinking hot day a week before, she had received a letter from her agent, Nina, asking when exactly she might have something new to show—read *sell*.

Maggie had sat curled up on a chair on her back veranda, playing with Smiley's big soft ears and staring through the top of her backyard growth at the hazy horizon beyond, and it had occurred to her for the first time that day that she might never produce anything worthy of selling again. Her vibrant, abstract portraits with their distinctive lashing swathes of primary colours and movement and mirth might well be a thing of the past, for now all she seemed able to produce were nondescript, unintelligible smudges of blue.

Even the pressure of Nina's letter, which hinted broadly at a parting of the ways if she didn't produce and soon, hadn't provided her with the stimulation she required, for out here it was physically impossible to build up a rich head of steam. Out here she needed something different to pull her out of her professional doldrums. Something special. She needed the possibility of a pure, unspoilt beach at the bottom of her cliff.

And for that she needed Tom Campbell. And his muscles. And his can do attitude. And his bright sunshiny contentment, no matter that it touched a raw nerve. That sounded like a plan.

She breathed in deep through her nose. 'If you need any more coffee, help yourself,' she said, backing up a step. 'Ditto on the contents of my fridge.'

As Maggie headed up the stairs, she was caught in a delicious wave of hot aftershave, hot coffee and hot sunshine rolling in from the coast.

And somehow that very mix of scents only served to remind her how quickly a person's best laid plans could unravel before their very eyes.

At the end of a long hot day grappling blackberries, lantana and what seemed like every other heinous weed known to man, Tom dusted himself off, collected his rags, tools and sweater and found his new employer in the corner of the great room, staring at her blue canvas with such concentration that he thought she might well find the answer to life, the universe and everything within its lumps and weaves.

His back muscles hurt. His forearms were scratched to hell. He was hot, filthy and lathered in sweat. Right then he'd gladly put life, the universe and everything on hold for the sake of a shower, a square meal and a cold beer.

As he neared, he saw that the red splatters from earlier had been cleared away. No, not cleared, but diffused into the blue, giving shade and depth where there had previously been none. He also realised that Maggie was humming.

Tom took another step, his boot-clad foot rolling heel, instep, toe, not yet ready to be discovered.

It was such a subtle sound it was more of a tuneful breath than a hum, but he was sure he recognised the song. Was it something classical? He was more of a classic rock fan himself, but he *knew* the tune. Or maybe he only recognised the feeling behind the husky, sonorous, faraway note threading from Maggie's throat and curling itself out into the room like the thin tendrils of smoke from a torch singer's cigarette.

Tom breathed it in, but it was too late before he realised his intake of breath was louder than her subdued singing.

Maggie turned from the hips, a skinny, dry paintbrush clenched between her teeth like a rose for a tango dancer.

'I'm done for the day,' he said, his right foot cocked guiltily.

She slid the paintbrush from between her teeth and blinked several times before he was entirely certain she remembered who he was and what he was doing there.

How's that for gratitude? he thought, placing his right foot and his sensibilities firmly on the ground.

'The backyard,' he said by way of a reminder, 'will take me over a week. Probably closer to two. And you were right about the chainsaw. We'll also need a skip to dispose of the mess so the spores won't bring it all back again by the end of the summer. My cousin Alex owns the hardware store in Rye, so I'll talk to him tomorrow and then I can give you a formal quote.'

'That's fine,' she said, her bare feet twisting until her legs caught up with her hips. 'Go ahead. Take the two weeks. Order the equipment. Do whatever it takes.'

'Are you sure you don't want to wait for my quote before deciding?'

'Positive. If you think you can do it, I want to go ahead. But if you would prefer I pay you upfront, I can give you some cash now,' she said, her gaze shifting to the edge of his face on the last couple of words. 'I have enough. Plenty.'

She made a move to step off her drop cloth but then stopped just as her toes scrunched around the edge. Her eyes shifted again until she looked him in the eye, and out of nowhere her sharp edges softened until all he could think of was mussed hair and long lean lines and winsome entreaty.

Tom was infinitely glad in that moment that she hadn't yet figured out that he was the man who couldn't say no. If she asked him to work through the night he wondered whether he might just turn around and head back out to the scratchy leaves.

'Oh no,' she said, blushing madly. 'I used the last of my cash on paint yesterday. Can I write you a cheque?'

'A cheque will be fine,' he said, his voice unusually gruff. He cleared his throat. 'There's no rush, though. You can hardly skip out on me. I know where you live.'

In order to ease some of the unexpected tension from the room, Tom winked and tried his charming smile on for size. But Maggie just blinked some more, those big grey eyes deep and unfathomable. If anything, she drew further inside herself, scrunching her toes into the grey sheet beneath her feet.

Tom had a sudden vision of Tess laughing herself silly at him—grinning and winking and flirting and making plans to wow the beguilingly aloof newcomer with his wit and charm—while the beguilingly aloof newcomer looked at him as if he was a piece of lint clogging what was surely a very nice view of the navel she so liked gazing at.

And Tess would have been in the right. The summer romance he had quite happily envisaged all morning wasn't going to happen. For Maggie smelled of Sonia Rykiel. And he smelled of sweat. She was a city girl doing an abominable job of pretending to be a beach girl, and he was a beach boy trying his best to pretend he'd never had a life anywhere else.

Her drop cloth said it all. She had no intention of leaving her mark—not on this house, not on this town and not on some cocky handyman flitting through her life.

'Ten a.m. tomorrow okay?' he asked, taking a step back.

'Ten a.m. Ten p.m. I'll be here, chained to my painting, trying to prise Smiley off my feet,' she said. Then from nowhere her cheek suddenly creased into the beginnings of a rueful grin and for a brief second she was engaging, not all that aloof, and downright gorgeous.

He took another deliberate step towards the front door. 'See you then, Maggie.'

'See you then, Tom.'

Tom turned and walked out the fern-laden front entrance, past the saddest-looking dog in the world and through the crumbling ruins of her front yard; he had the feeling he would never forget any odd detail of meeting Maggie Bryce, no matter how she might wish him to do so.

CHAPTER THREE

THE next morning Tom parked at the back of Maggie's house on the dot of ten, the tray of his truck filled with all sorts of weird and wonderful appliances borrowed from Alex's hardware store.

In a repeat of the day before, Smiley lifted his head for a scratch behind the ear when Tom met him at the front door, and inside Lady Bryce was to be found staring at her painting.

Overnight Tom had managed to talk down the potency of the impact she'd made on him, putting it all down to becoming overcome with paint fumes. But seeing her in the flesh again, he had to admit that, despite the insomnia and lack of furniture, and issues the likes of which a determinedly casual guy like he had no intention of getting mixed up in, she truly was an enchanting soul.

She was dressed down again, this time in a yellow hooded top and dark brown cargoes, her dust-coloured hair pulled back into a messy ponytail and held back by a red bandanna, but beneath it all she had the posture of a princess.

Add to that her dark and delicious scent that bombarded him the second he walked inside her front door, and Tom knew that if she ever let down that prickly guard of hers for longer than ten seconds over a stale cheese and tomato sandwich, Lady Bryce would be some package.

His gaze slid sideways to the big blue painting. To his eyes it was exactly how he remembered it. No progress had been made.

He'd never tried to paint a picture since primary school, but he knew enough about creativity to know there was more to a lack of inspiration than the need for a deadline. Having to produce a finished painting of a tree by the end of class hadn't made him an artist.

But then again Maggie *was* different. Different from him, anyway. Didn't she crave male company besides that of a glum canine? And something else to drink besides coffee? And furniture? Didn't she crave furniture? Why *did* she have no furniture?

The more the questions about Maggie mounted, the more he wanted to know the answers. All the answers. Like how she could still be so dumbfoundingly immune to his smiles and why, despite her reserve, he still cared.

'Morning, Maggie,' he said a mite louder than necessary.

When she spun to face him he was pleased to see that it only took about a second for her to remember exactly who he was.

'Oh, good morning, Tom.' She had dark smudges of grey beneath her eyes and if she wasn't in a different outfit he might have guessed that she'd pulled an all-nighter. Though the three coffee mugs lined up behind her water jars told a different story. 'How did you go with your supplies?'

'Great. I'm all ready to make a go of it.'

'Coffee?' she asked, already moving off her drop cloth and towards the long skinny kitchen.

'You bet.'

'Did you get the chance to formalise the quote?' she asked as she tucked her bandanna into the back pocket of her cargo pants, shook out her long ponytail and retied it, scrubbed her hands clean, then put the kettle on to boil.

They agreed on a time limit—two weeks, and a price—

enough to keep Tom in hot dinners for the next month even if the ocean ran dry of fish, and enough that he noticed a rapid widening of Maggie's soft grey eyes despite the fact that she didn't hesitate to reach straight for her cheque book from an otherwise bare kitchen drawer.

Tom held up both hands. 'How about we save all that for the last day?'

Her eyes narrowed, as though trying to figure out how he was planning to screw her over.

'It's probably not the best business practice,' he said, 'but I've found it helps keeps relations friendly. This way I get treated like a helpful guest rather than having to deal with the odd situation of working for a friend.'

'If you're sure you'd prefer it that way,' she said, turning away from him, closing the cheque book and sliding it into the empty kitchen drawer.

'I do. After all's said and done, we exchange a discreet envelope and a handshake before organising the next bowling outing or dinner invite.'

Her eyes widened ever so slightly. Did she think he was hitting on her? Had he accidentally given himself an avenue to do so?

Tom wondered what Maggie might say if he made the dinner invite suggestion concrete. Maybe something casual at his place with another couple to keep it relaxed. Alex and Marianne were always good for a laugh when you could get them away from their brood of five girls under the age of eight.

A heavy furry lump landed upon Tom's toes. And the moment was gone.

'Smiley, come on,' Maggie said, clicking her fingers at the despondent-looking creature. But Smiley wasn't silly. He could play deaf with the best of them.

'I'm sorry,' she said, her cheek twitching. 'You could try giving him a little shove.'

But Smiley let his chin slump on to his crossed front legs with a great rush of air streaming from his nostrils. He wasn't going anywhere.

'Sorry,' she said again. 'He spends half his day sitting on my toes. He looks miserable but really he's just a big mushy bundle of love.'

Tom smiled. 'It's fine.'

She took a step closer and clicked madly at the dog. And over the scent of Smiley, Tom once more caught a wave of Maggie's perfume. For a woman who wore not a lick of make-up and so clearly didn't feel the need to dress up for him, the aesthetic nature of that elegant scent was an anomaly.

And anomalies were intriguing. Even to the most invulnerable of men. Search and discover—it was as instinctive to the human male as breathing.

Maybe inviting her to dinner wouldn't be such a bad idea after all. But without the chaperons. Candlelight. No, moonlight. On his back deck. Fresh calamari, barbecued. And a cold liberating beer to wash it all down...

Maggie moved closer still, bent down to her haunches and looked Smiley in the eye. Though Tom was sure the dog knew it for the ruse it was, he hauled his great hulking form off the floor and padded over to his mistress for a big cuddle before heading over to sit in the kitchen doorway.

The walking talking anomaly in question stood, and suddenly there was nothing between the two of them bar a metre of space and warm swirls of hot spring sea air. He saw the moment Maggie knew it too. Her mouth slowly turned downwards and she thrust her hands in her back pockets.

Tom's instincts hollered at him to hunt and gather. To

smile, to flirt, to grow a backbone and simply ask her out. What was so important about furniture, really?

But every lick of sense in his body told him to leave well enough alone and get back to work. Despite the bare feet and mussed hair, this woman wasn't in the same place he was. She was haughty and urbane, all sharp edges and scepticism. His head *knew* that would hardly make for a fun date. If only his impulses were half as rational.

Tom downed the remainder of his black coffee in one hit, thus negating every scent bar the strong roasted beans. He rinsed the mug and left it upside down on the sink and moved out of the skinny kitchen.

'What time would you like lunch?' Maggie called out before he got as far as the back door.

He turned to find her standing in the kitchen doorway, her long length leaning against the door jamb, her fingers unconsciously running up and down Smiley's forehead and curling about his ears.

And though he had a bunch of ham and avocado sandwiches, fruit and a block of dark chocolate in a cooler in his truck, Tom found himself saying, 'Whenever you're having yours.'

As he walked down the back steps he didn't look back. He didn't need to. He could feel her guarded grey eyes watching him all the way.

Maggie's work in progress was going nowhere fast. And considering she spent all day every day looking out over one of the most inspirational views any artist could hope to find— well, bar whomever Michelangelo based the David upon—it was frustrating as hell.

True she hadn't painted a landscape in years. Her talent had always run to portraits. From the first picture she'd ever painted for her dad when she was four years old to grade school art class, to her art school scholarship days, to her first showing and onwards.

But when she'd first moved to Portsea she hadn't been able to shrug off a few particular faces that she had no intention of painting. So she'd decided to try her hand at something new, something innocuous, something safe: landscapes. But so far they all had the emotional impact of a pot plant.

Rubbing a hand over her tight neck muscles, she stepped off her cloth and let her body flop forward until her hands were touching the ground. As the blood rushed to her head, mercifully blocking out the faces therein, Maggie heard a strain of something familiar tickle at the back of her mind.

She stood up so fast she almost blacked out, but the sound was still there. Music. She'd heard music.

Drawn to the sound like scattered iron filings to a magnet, she followed it down the back steps and around the side of the house, to find Tom sitting on the flat bed of his truck with a grindstone in one hand and a set of garden shears in the other. A small black radio roosted atop the cab of his truck, blaring out an early INXS song.

Maggie stayed in the shadows, watching as Tom sharpened the shears, the muscles along his back clenching with a measured rhythm. There was nothing rushed about the way he worked, as though his time was his alone.

She only *wished* she could be that laid-back. She'd tried, really she had, going with the Wednesday girls to wine and cheese clubs and early morning t'ai chi on the beach. But all she'd wanted to do afterwards was indulge in a healthy dose of road rage or to scream at the referees at a footy match to relieve the tension build-up in her head.

Freya had suggested she ought to blame it all on her

deadbeat dad and that hypnotherapy would help. Maggie thought it more likely she was suffering from withdrawal from the little cherry and white chocolate muffins she used to buy from the café below her apartment every Sunday.

But there was Tom, a Sydney guy oozing a kind of laid-back charm that Maggie had believed she could never achieve even after a million years of t'ai chi. So how did he come to be that relaxed? Melbourne was a challenging city, but Sydney was ten times so.

Unless of course she was thinking about it all wrong. Maybe he'd always been mellow and had never quite had it in him to run the rat race and that was why he'd moved to Sorrento when his sister no longer needed him there. She wasn't sure if that thought made her feel better or worse.

She must have made a noise. Or perhaps Tom had sensed her watching him. Either way, he turned, pinning her with that hot hazel gaze. He watched her for a few moments, giving away nothing, before his shoulders relaxed, an easy smile melted away all earlier single-minded concentration and Tom the laid-back charmer was back.

'Howdy,' he drawled.

'Hi,' she said, her voice strangely breathy.

'What's up?'

She came away from her hiding place, placing her bare feet carefully as she walked to avoid the prickles. 'I heard music.'

Tom closed one eye and squinted over his shoulder at his stereo. 'It's not too loud, is it?'

She shook her head. 'Not at all. I love this song. I haven't heard it since I was a teenager.'

Tom reached over and turned the stereo up a fraction and Maggie felt the familiar assertive beat pulsing more strongly through her veins with every footfall.

'I used to always have music playing in the background when I worked,' she said. 'Though it was usually classical CDs. Sometimes I would get one piece in my head and I had to listen to it over and over for weeks while I worked on a particular painting. It drove everyone else mad.'

Her voice faded and she waited for him to enquire as to whom the 'everyone else' might be, but he merely looked up at her with that carefree, smiling face of his. Such a nice face, she thought—lots of character. The kind of face that would light well, easily capturing shadows and allowing those intelligent eyes to become the focus of the piece. Not that she had any intention of painting the guy, ever.

'I've got this song on CD. I could lend it to you.'

'I could probably do with all the help I can get right now,' she admitted. And it was a pretty nice song actually. Moody. Evocative.

'Have you got an iPod?' he asked.

She shook her head. She had once. She wished then that she'd thought to bring it with her when she'd left Melbourne. But she'd been in such a terrible hurry that night, such a blinding self-directed rage, and all she'd been thinking of was the need to get away…

Maybe a small second-hand stereo wouldn't be such a stretch. She could shift the dial a centimetre to the left from where it usually rested and it might make all the difference. A new music station for a new place. A new song for a new painting.

'So why do you need help?' Tom asked.

'My painting sucks,' she shot back, and felt as surprised as he looked. 'Wow, I can't believe I just said that out loud. I've never told anyone when I've felt blocked before.'

'Why on earth not?' he asked. 'Everyone's allowed to have a down patch every now and then.'

'Once it's out there,' she said, 'you can never take it back. Like if I ever *said* my painting sucked, then that would make it so.'

It occurred to Maggie that she had given her life the same treatment—smiling her way through the down patches, only pouring out her feelings on to the canvas, and look where that had landed her. Alone, all but broke and drooling over the idea of buying a second-hand stereo.

Tom lowered his shears and shuffled his backside sideways, leaving a space for her to sit beside him if she so desired. And it didn't take much thought for her to decide that she did.

She placed a hand on the hot metal tray and lifted herself up. Tom's feet touched the ground but she had to point her toes to touch dirt. She gave up and let her long legs swing free.

'I like it,' he said. 'Your painting.'

She turned her head an inch and squinted up at him, to find that those dark hazel eyes were even more intimidating up close and personal. It made her feel slightly unsettled.

'No, you don't,' she said.

'Sure I do. Blue's my favourite colour,' he insisted. 'And your painting has a lot of blue in it. So far there's nothing about it for me *not* to like.' His mouth didn't need to move for her to know that he was smiling inside.

'Heathen,' she said, rolling her eyes, and turning away to hide her own budding smile.

After a few moments of collective silence, Tom asked, 'So what is it a painting of, exactly?'

Maggie laughed, the sensation decompressing her a little. Her feet stopped swinging. Her hands unclenched from the edge of the truck's tray. And her shoulders lowered a good inch.

She went to tell him it was the vista out of her window, but even she knew it wasn't that. It wasn't even nearly close to being that. 'It's the last in a long line of paintings of a blue smudge,' she said. 'And, since you like blue so very much, if you want it you can have it.'

He glanced at her and then he nodded. 'Deal. But only if we agree that I can have The Big Blue in lieu of payment.'

Maggie opened her mouth to argue, to ask how he could survive on her job alone if he wasn't getting paid for it, but the devil on her shoulder screamed at her to take the deal. The money she'd earmarked would come in more handy to her than she would ever admit out loud. But the angel on her other shoulder gently reminded her she'd been kidding when she'd made the offer.

'It's a deal-breaker,' Tom said before she could get a word in. 'I get the painting or the dough. I won't accept both.'

Maggie closed her eye to the angel and said, 'Okay. Deal.' Heck, if they'd made the same arrangement a year before he would have come out the better by far. It wasn't her fault his timing was unlucky.

Tom leaned back, away from her, so that he could make sure she was really looking at him. 'But it's not finished yet, is it?'

'How can you tell?'

'You wouldn't spend so much time staring at the thing if you were done with it, would you?' he asked.

She shrugged and looked up the grassy hill towards her front gate, not at all equipped for this stranger, this man, to know her quite so well so quickly.

'So go on,' he said. 'You've given me two weeks to get this mess of a backyard cleaned up. I'll give you the same two weeks to finish my painting.'

'Two weeks? At the rate I'm going, I reckon it's going to take more like two years.'

Tom's bottom lip jutted out as he absorbed this new piece

of information. 'I thought I remembered you telling me you work better under pressure.'

Maggie felt a smile tugging at the corner of her mouth but she kept her gaze dead ahead. 'Was that me?'

'It was. So consider this pressure. But because I think you drink too much coffee, and I'd like you to get some sleep during that time, I'll let you off the hook just a little. I'll still be here in two years, so if that's what it will take, that's what it'll take.'

Maggie blinked. Imagining where she would be two weeks into the future was quite enough to grasp, but two years? Two years ago she was living on another planet, living another person's life. Two years ago she was the toast of the town, selling faster than any other fine artist in Australia, happily married, or so she'd thought…

She took in a deep breath and looked around her. Salty sea air tickled the back of her nose. The distant sound of circling seagulls split the air. A big, beautiful, unconventional house disintegrated silently beside her, while a disturbingly charismatic man she barely knew sat all too comfortably a bare inch to her left. So whose life was she living now?

With a heartfelt sigh that was a million miles from contented, she slid slowly off the back of the truck and took a couple of steps back towards the house.

'Off in search of more distractions?' Tom asked. There was a definite twinkle in his eye that Maggie chose to ignore, for this guy was already becoming the kind of distraction she oughtn't to indulge in.

'Always. So you really think I can have this painting done in two weeks?' she asked, walking backwards.

He grinned and nodded. 'Somebody once told me there's nothing like a deadline to get a person inspired.'

Maggie gave him a smile, one that she felt bubble up from

some long buried place inside her, before she sauntered back to the house, humming a lively tune.

'I don't know what you're grizzling about. It's great.'

Later that afternoon Maggie blinked frantically to pull herself out of the gold and indigo smeared horizon to find Tom walking towards her, a mug of freshly brewed coffee in his hands.

'I'm sorry?'

'The Big Blue. He's coming along nicely.'

She twirled a thin, dry paintbrush between her fingers as she watched Tom's eyes flicker appreciatively over the large canvas. That afternoon she'd added some colourful smears to the upper half, so though it still mightn't be any good, or any *thing*, at least it was progress.

Tom moved to stand beside her, so close Maggie could feel heat waves emanating from his sun-drenched skin. His heavy work boots half disappeared into the folds of her huge drop cloth. He brought his coffee to his mouth and took a swig, but his eyes never once left the painting.

Her stomach took a small happy trip as she experienced the thrill that came with seeing someone making a connection with one of her paintings.

'It's really growing on me,' he said. 'Yep, this one's going to look just right on the wall in my john.'

Maggie coughed out a laugh. It was so without warning that her stomach kind of clenched. The sensation wasn't in any way uncomfortable but it made her feel off kilter all the same. She crossed her arms low over her belly.

'If you're even thinking about putting this painting on your toilet wall, Tom Campbell, the deal's off.'

'Fine,' he said. 'Okay. Though more people would get to enjoy it there than anywhere else in my house.'

He turned to face her so quickly she hoped he didn't realise she had been staring at him rather than the subject of their conversation. She glanced away quickly, but not before she'd noticed the solid crease appear above the corner of his mouth.

'I'm kind of glad my agent won't get to see this one,' she admitted.

'You have an agent?'

She faced him fully and glared. 'I thought we had decided you thought I was talented.'

He laughed, his eyes creasing, every part of him seeming to overflow with amusement. Beneath her crossed arms it now felt as though her stomach had flipped all the way over.

'Sorry,' he said, his eyes dancing. 'Of course we had. That came out wrong. It's just that we get painters out here all the time. In summer they line the beaches, painting beach huts and sunsets over Sorrento. But I just never knew anybody personally who'd actually sold anything.'

Maggie shrugged. 'Well, now you do.'

Tom nodded, kept watching her, and she felt the word *personally* dig into her mind and take hold. She let her arms drop, then began twirling the paintbrush again to give herself something to do with her suddenly nervy hands.

'How do you do that?' he asked, shifting closer and glancing at her hand.

'It's easy,' she said. 'Much easier than actually painting, therefore one of the all-time great distractions.'

He held out a hand. 'Show me how?'

Maggie stopped twirling, clamping the wood into a closed fist. She dropped the brush into Tom's open palm, careful not to let her fingers touch his.

He looked down the barrel of the brush for any aerodynamic imperfections, weighed it in his palm, then held it between his forefinger and his thumb, swinging it back and forth, as though the brush would give into his mighty will and perform the trick on its own.

'It's physically impossible,' he finally said. 'It's too long to fit between the gaps in my fingers.'

'Oh, rubbish.' Maggie plucked a larger brush from her stash and tucked it between her first and middle fingers. 'It has nothing to do with physics and everything to do with faith.'

As she'd done a hundred times before when art students had asked her the same thing, she looked him in the eye and waited until all of his attention was focused there. Okay, so maybe that wasn't her brightest idea. For some reason his hazel eyes did things to her insides that art students' eyes never had. Her hand began to shake.

Better to get it over with then, she thought. She took a shallow breath and started to spin.

'Hey!' he called out. Naturally he'd been looking the wrong way and had missed the trick entirely.

She finished her twirl with a flourish, spun the brush into the air and caught it behind her back.

'Holy moly.' He blinked, amazed, and she felt her cheeks warming under his blatant appraisal. 'I can see now how many hours of seeking distractions can produce artistry all of their own.'

Tom went to put the brush back on to her table, but before she knew what she was doing, Maggie reached out, about to clamp down on his wrist. But she stopped herself just in time, her hand hovering so close to his skin she could feel the hairs on his arms rising to meet her.

He stilled and looked back at her. His eyes were no longer smiling, now questioning.

'Keep it,' she said, her voice coming out unnaturally low.

She pulled her hand back into its safety zone in the back pocket of her cargo pants. 'You need the practice.'

He nodded. 'Thanks.'

When he stepped off her drop cloth Maggie felt a huge weight rise off her chest. She realised then that she hadn't taken a proper breath since the moment he'd walked in the room.

'I'll be off, then,' he said. 'And don't argue, but tomorrow lunch is my treat.'

'Who's arguing?' Maggie said.

He saluted her with the paintbrush she had given him, then jogged out the front door and was gone.

And, with a ragged sigh, Maggie knew that neither his empty coffee cup resting on her paint table, nor the paintbrush now missing from her jar would be the reasons she thought of him often before she went to sleep much much later that night.

CHAPTER FOUR

TOM twirled his keys around his finger as he walked up to the front door of his bungalow. He spun around on the spot in a move that would have made John Travolta proud, before sliding the key into the front door.

Once inside he tossed his car keys into a small wooden bowl on his antique Queen Anne hall table and immediately thought of the dilapidated garden bench that served as Maggie's hall table.

That was one interesting woman. Smart. Sharp. Deep as a well. And *funny*. The last thing he would have expected Maggie to be was funny. In his book, sharp and funny was a killer cocktail.

He listened to his answering machine messages with half an ear as a few job offers came in. But he would happily pass them off to someone else, as for the next two weeks he was a contentedly kept man.

He flicked a wall switch that lit up the several large lamps in his great room in one go. His dark leather sofas, mahogany side tables, shiny wooden floors and collection of fine art warmed under the golden glow.

It sure was different from Maggie's great room. He no longer lived in the exclusive North Shore of Sydney, and he now worked as a handyman rather than as the head of a multi-billion dollar restoration company, but that didn't mean he couldn't surround himself with the finer things he'd been able to amass while making his fortune. So what *was* stopping her from filling her big old house with any furniture at all?

He'd have a shower and a beer before making himself a pasta dinner, and he could think on all that for a few hours in front of the footy channel…

'Evening, Tom.' The outline of a man lit by the blue glow of the laptop screen in Tom's office made him jump fair out of his skin.

'Alex!' he cried out. 'Make yourself known a little earlier next time, why don't you?'

'Sorry, Cuz,' Alex said. 'You know how it is. Head down, bum on seat, working hard. Internet is down at the office and I needed to place a couple of last-minute orders. Hope you don't mind.'

'Of course I don't mind. Do you want a beer?'

'I'm good.' Without looking away from the laptop, Alex reached out and grabbed the half empty bottle at his side.

'So what's on the agenda at your place tonight?' Tom asked as he moved into the raised kitchen to get his own cold drink.

'Music lessons. Dora's taken up the trumpet,' Alex admitted. Tom laughed. He was pretty certain the last-minute orders for the hardware store were not all that urgent.

'So how did it go with Lady Bryce today?' Alex asked. 'What's she like? A recluse? Or just snobby, as the Barclays seem to think? Did you need the chainsaw for the job or was that just an insurance policy?'

'None of the above, actually. Maggie is perfectly amiable.' Well, not *perfectly*, but he'd discovered that she at least knew how to be.

'Hang on a cotton pickin' minute, Tommy Boy,' Alex said, spinning on Tom's office chair to face him with a grin spread across his round friendly face, all urgent orders forgotten. 'Did I hear a note of appreciation in your voice?'

Tommy Boy was about to deny it, but there was no getting around Alex. The poor guy lived in a house surrounded by women. Even his daughter's pet rabbits were female. Alex looked to Tom for manly succour. And Tom looked to Alex as his only remaining family. How could he let him down?

'I'm afraid you do, Alex. For there is much to appreciate about my good lady employer.'

'Don't tell me she's hot,' Alex insisted.

Tom baulked at the implication. *Hot* was completely the wrong word for Maggie Bryce. If anything she was too cool. Friendly but reticent. Inquisitive but isolated. Like a bird that had had her wings clipped.

'She's intriguing,' Tom allowed.

'Right,' Alex said, his disappointment at her not being an undercover Playboy bunny all too evident.

'And it can't have even been our third conversation when I told her about Tess,' Tom admitted before he'd even felt the words forming. He took another long sip of his beer as he waited for Alex's gaping mouth to snap shut.

'And why was that, do you think?' his cousin eventually asked.

'I have not one single clue.'

'Does she…remind you of Tess?'

Tom shrugged. 'Not all that much. She's graceful, like a ballet dancer. Tess was a pipsqueak and a tomboy who'd never quite lost her baby fat. But Maggie's a painter and you know Tess was a big art lover. Maybe that's what made me mention her.'

He looked to Alex, who merely shrugged.

'But she is plucky. She has a wicked tongue on her. Pretty sarcastic at times. Tess would have loved that.'

Everyone could do with a bit of spice in their diet, Tom thought, taking another swig of his beer. But he and Tess had always prized it more than most. Tom still missed their sparring matches. Every single day…

'So what's her first name again?'

'Hmm?' Tom said, breathing deep through his nose.

'The painter with the wicked tongue.'

'Maggie,' Tom said.

And then suddenly Alex was facing the computer and typing again.

'What are you doing?'

'Googling her,' Alex said.

Knowing it was wrong, and spying, and intrusive, Tom moved to look over Alex's shoulder.

'Well,' Alex said, 'according to *Google*, Maggie Bryce is a thirteen-year-old skateboarding champ from Canberra, or a ninety-four-year-old horse strapper in Ireland. I could try adding *intriguing* and *sarcastic* as qualifiers but I'm not sure that'd help.'

'May I?' Tom asked as he motioned to his desk, his chair and his laptop.

'Of course.' Alex squeezed his large form from the chair and let Tom sit. He leaned over, breathing down Tom's neck. 'This is too much fun.'

'You need to get out more.'

'And don't I know it.'

Tom added 'Melbourne painter' to the search parameters and he found her. He found pictures of her in her late teens, beaming at the camera while standing next to a vibrant, colourful portrait of her art teacher after winning…the Archibald Prize?

Tom sat against the back of his chair with a thud. There was no doubting it was her. The ear to ear grin was something Tom hadn't witnessed as yet but the biscuit-blonde hair, the dancer's grace and those wide grey eyes were unmistakable.

'Sheesh,' Alex whistled in his ear. 'That Archibald thing's a big deal, right?'

'About as big a deal as it can get,' Tom said.

He clicked on another site to find her a few years down the track, looking more like herself—dressed in a T-shirt and jeans with a splotch of paint on her cheek as she taught art to a large group of pre-schoolers. But again she was grinning, all high cheekbones and comely overbite.

'What are you talking about?' Alex said. 'She's more than just intriguing, my friend. She's beautiful.'

Beautiful. That was the word he'd been looking for. Nothing as crass and undignified as *hot*. Or as forbidding as *cool*. Maggie Bryce was beautiful.

Tom shuffled in his seat and made himself concentrate. He clicked on yet another website, which showed pictures of her at a gallery opening in Armadale. The gallery had shown several of her paintings, all of them selling for amounts so astronomical Alex coughed so hard he had to take a moment to get another beer.

In those pictures the money that afforded her a home in Portsea showed. Her hair was ice blonde and cut into a slick do that tucked perfectly along her cheekbones and flicked beneath her chin. She wore ubiquitous Melbourne black that made her look tall and slim, but still more curvaceous than she was now.

But in these pictures she wasn't smiling any more. Her eyes were sadder somehow. Older. The shining light that had turned her eyes to molten silver in that school room picture had dimmed.

He scrolled down the page. But she was only in the background of a couple more pictures with a good-looking guy with salt-and-pepper hair, bent over, listening to him and touching him on the arm. The level of attention she was giving to the guy was enough to have him slam his laptop closed.

'Hey!' Alex cried out.

'That's enough,' Tom insisted. 'You've seen what she looks like, you know she's a hot-shot painter, now you know all I know about her.'

Alex laughed and moved away, taking his beer with him. '*Now* I know why she has you all hot and bothered. Miss Hoity-Toity treats you as Tom the handyman, doesn't she?'

Tom ran a hand over his rough chin. 'I *am* Tom the handyman,' he insisted. 'I have been for years.'

'Have you told her what you used to do for a living?'

'Not in detail. But she's upstairs painting and I'm downstairs wielding sharp, dangerous cutting implements. There's not much time for small talk.'

Tom had never hidden the fact that he had money. Those close to him knew, and thought it a great lark that he'd downgraded his skill set to changing light bulbs rather than ordering them by the hundreds for the intricate restoration of old buildings. It made it easier having the locals know too as they didn't mind sending work to other people or calling off jobs late, which was fine with him. But he'd never run around with a megaphone telling every newcomer either.

So where did that leave Maggie?

Alex slumped down into a plush wing-chair by the desk. 'I would put money on the fact that when around pretty little Lady Bryce, the big-shot, CEO, he-man inside of you just itches to come out of his cave and beat his chest.'

'She's not little,' Tom said. 'She's taller than you.'

That shut Alex up, just as he'd hoped.

'And you're nowhere near the mark,' Tom said, stalking over to the remote to turn on his wide-screen TV. 'She's a job, that's all. Just as restoring old homes was just a job. Nothing more than a means to an end.'

He took a moment to gulp down a swig of beer.

Alex reached out and gave him a slap on the back. He knew better than anyone that the reason Tom had made Campbell Designs such a phenomenal success had been to make enough money to get Tess the best medical treatment money could buy.

'And when I've reached the end of this job,' Tom continued, 'Maggie'll be another face driving past in the street and I'll be just another name in the Peninsula phone book.'

But if Alex knew that the end had become the ownership of a big smudge of blue on canvas, he would laugh until beer came out of his nose.

Late the next morning, a bustle of noise at Maggie's front door heralded the arrival of Freya, Sandra and Ashleigh, the Wednesday girls. Annoyed at the racket, Smiley plodded through the house and out the back door.

Sandra, the youngest of the gang, lumbered in first, her dark wavy hair in pigtails, her pretty blue eyes rimmed in lashings of rebellious black kohl and her heavy combat boots clumping loudly on the wooden floor.

'Mornin', Mags, sorry we're late. Blame Freya,' she called out, dumping her black leather beanbag in the middle of the floor.

Freya, a single mum with twin girls in the first grade, whirled in next, short red hair scruffy, pale cheeks pink, clay stains on her freckled arms, carrying a huge tartan picnic blanket and a cooler filled with gourmet foods.

'Read the thing or don't read the thing,' Freya shouted over her shoulder. 'I don't care. You're always going on about male domination in the creation of modern religion and this book says much the same.'

Freya waved a dog-eared copy of *The Da Vinci Code* over her shoulder like a waggling finger at the third musketeer, Ashleigh, Maggie's old art teacher, the patron of the group and the eldest at somewhere over fifty years old. Well over, Maggie guessed, though with her short, insanely curly ash-blonde hair and layers of autumnal-coloured clothes, she had always seemed kind of ageless.

Ashleigh smiled serenely at Maggie and carried an Edwardian dining chair in her elegant wake, before her pale eyes swayed to the painting over her shoulder. Her gaze wandered carefully over the piece, then down to the floor where the dozen other members of the lukewarm Blue Smudge Series rested haphazardly against one another.

Ashleigh hooked a long thin hand through Maggie's elbow. 'This new one's coming along nicely, don't you think?'

Maggie didn't think any such thing. 'Wine for everyone?' she called out rather than saying so.

'God, yes,' Freya gasped, heading into the kitchen.

'Make mine a double,' Sandra said, shuffling a French cigarette from a box as she stared at Maggie's painting, with her forehead creased into a kind of determined concentration only the young could achieve without leaving a mark.

'So what's it all about?' Sandra asked, her hand hovering an inch from the canvas as though it could communicate better to her that way.

'Beats me,' Maggie admitted. 'But it has a name now at least. The Big Blue.' When the younger woman tossed a cigarette into her mouth Maggie said, 'Take it outside.'

'Right,' Sandra said through a curled lip as she flicked her hot pink bra strap back under the thin strap of her black tank top and disappeared out on to the veranda.

Maggie and Ashleigh shared a look. 'Do you remember ever being that young?' Maggie asked.

'I was never that young,' Ashleigh said.

Freya came back from the kitchen with three full wine-glasses. 'So what are you working on?' she asked.

Maggie pointed over her shoulder and Freya turned, focused and saw it in all its obviousness. 'Right. Okay. But it's a landscape.'

Maggie felt both women's eyes zero in on her. She could tell them she thought it sucked too, right? These were her friends, her kindred spirits, her peers, and the ones who had taken her in and held her close six months before when her life had fallen apart.

'It *is* a landscape,' she said optimistically. 'I'm trying something new.'

Freya frowned. 'Really? I mean, is that wise at this point in your career?'

Ashleigh must have given Freya *the look*, for the colour brightened in her freckled cheeks. '*What*? Just because you enjoy being a tortured artist doesn't mean that some of us don't quite like the fact that we've beaten the odds and made a fine living at it.'

Freya lumped Ashleigh with the wineglasses and took Maggie by the hands. 'Maggie, it would be like a children's book author deciding to write erotic thrillers. Risky as all get out.'

Maggie squeezed back. 'I don't think I have much choice, Freya. I think I'm all *portraited* out.'

Freya gave her a small smile, but Maggie knew that she wouldn't really understand. To Freya it was a nine-to-five job. But for Maggie, and for Ashleigh too, it had always been a little more magical than that. Art was a way of expressing her feelings—good and bad. And, on the flipside, it was that much harder when the expression dried up.

'Paint that!' Sandra gasped from the veranda. Through the window Maggie saw her pointing downwards with her smouldering cigarette. And then the sound of a chainsaw cut through the silence.

'Oh, shoot…' Before Maggie could think of an excuse to stop them, the other two women sorted out their wineglasses and headed outside. She had no choice but to follow.

'This is new,' Ashleigh rumbled under her breath.

Below, Tom stood with his legs shoulder-width apart as he wielded his chainsaw. Jeans hugged lean hips. His dark hair was spiky and a mess. And a sheen of sweat glowed along his tanned muscular arms.

Sandra sighed eloquently beside her and Maggie had to admit, even though she had been steadfastly paying no heed to the fact for days, he did make for quite the glorious picture.

'I know about him,' Freya said, her voice heavy with accusation. 'That's Tom Campbell. What's he doing here?'

Maggie leant away from the rail and moved back inside; the last thing she wanted was to be discovered ogling. The others followed after a time. Except one.

'Sandra,' Ashleigh called out, clicking her fingers.

Sandra took a drag on her cigarette, put it out in a potted fern, took one last lingering look at Tom, then clumped back in.

Maggie grabbed a fat cushion from its hidey hole behind her easel and threw it on to the floor, then took a seat. When the others made it to their respective places she elaborated. 'He's just doing some work around the garden.'

Sandra's pierced right eyebrow shot into a perfect V.

'Can you really see *me* out there working a chainsaw?' Maggie asked. 'I can barely work a stovetop, much less a complex piece of machinery. And when I looked him up in the local phone book under 'H' for Handyman, I had no idea *that* was going to turn up. Truly.'

'Likely tale,' Sandra said, leaning back into her beanbag.

'Maggie, I thought we had all agreed that you are meant to be reconnecting with your art and with yourself,' Freya said, 'not *connecting* with some musclebound hunk.'

But I'm not connecting with anything! Maggie wanted to scream. *I feel so disconnected. From my life. From my home. From the artistic expression which sustained me for the last ten years.*

But they had tried so hard to include her, to encourage her, to promise her that beach life would make it all better; how could she tell them it wasn't working?

'So you think he's hunky, hey, Freya?' Sandra asked.

'What I *know*,' Freya said, 'is that he spent last summer with that divorced American broad who spent her whole time here telling everyone who would listen that she got Mornington Manor in a divorce and couldn't wait to sell the "quaint little house on the bluff" so she could move back to California.'

'So he dated someone and it didn't work out,' Sandra said, saying the words Maggie ought to have come up with, if she hadn't been so distracted by trying to imagine what the American broad might have looked like.

'We've all been there,' Sandra said. 'And, as to the American, you just didn't like her because she called one of your pots "cute". Half the holiday houses on the Peninsula have come to the current owner in a divorce. Look at Maggie!'

Everyone did as Sandra suggested while Maggie took a rather large sip of her wine and declined to comment.

'This place was always hers, right?'

Maggie nodded.

'And at least *she* has no intention of selling and moving back to Melbourne when the bastard finally signs the papers,' Freya pointed out.

And again Maggie kept her mouth tight shut.

They were in a particularly feisty mood today and Maggie decided that if she opened up and told them exactly how dire her financial situation had become since she'd cut herself off, they'd be unbearable. Today she just wanted good wine, and good food, and noisy company. She was simply too tired for anything else.

'Well, now we've figured this Tom guy is now single,' Sandra said, 'who says Maggie doesn't deserve her own fling?'

'Sandra!' Freya shouted.

'I'd hazard a guess it's been a while since our Maggie has been flung. If ever,' Sandra continued unabated. 'Have you ever been flung, Maggie-Moo?'

One thing Maggie-Moo hadn't ever been was flung. She'd been a good daughter, a caring girlfriend and a loving wife. And had been let down on all counts. Until the day came when someone could promise her a fling would end any differently, she would remain unflung.

She tucked her legs beneath her and sat up straighter. 'I'm here to *work*, ladies,' she said, 'and to take a little time for me, just as Freya said. Not to be flung, or flinged or whatever the correct grammar for such a thing might be. Tom's here for another week and a half and then he's off to be someone else's handyman.'

'In the meantime, he's *your* handyman,' Sandra said.

'In the meantime nothing. End of discussion.'

Sandra harrumphed and pouted. Freya gave a self-satisfied

smile. And Maggie noticed that Ashleigh had been dead quiet throughout.

'So,' Maggie said, purposely avoiding Ashleigh's pale piercing eyes. 'Someone else's turn in the hot seat. Progress report. What are we all working on this week?'

Tom turned off the chainsaw. The late spring sun beat down on his back. His muscles ached. He was sweating so much he wished that the way to Maggie's potential beach was already clear so he could run down the steps and straight into the surf below.

But, despite the thick clustering branches still between him and the big blue sea, all in all he felt mighty good. Mighty pleased with himself. And mighty hungry.

It was after midday. He was surprised Maggie hadn't come down at some stage that morning. With coffee. Or with an excuse for a chat.

What was going on in that tangled mind of hers this fine day? He looked up at the large windows in Maggie's great room, but the sun only created an opaque reflection of ocean and scrub.

He wiped his hand on an old rag and straightened his T-shirt as much as he could, then jogged up the stairs, two at a time.

Maybe today he could ask her more about her career. That would be a neat segue into offering to make dinner at his place, where he could show off his collection, including the Sidney Nolan in his bedroom. Hey, that could be his opening line: *Come up to my place and check out my Nolan.*

Grinning, Tom called out, 'Hey, Maggie, I've got leftover fettuccini in the fridge. Prepare your tastebuds—'

But he stopped short when he found himself face to face with Maggie's back while three other women, all sitting in various stages of repose on an odd assortment of seats, all drinking red wine, all looked back at him with varying levels of interest.

'Afternoon, ladies,' he said.

At the sound of his voice, Maggie scrambled to her feet. 'Tom! Hi. Umm. Heck, what's the time? Is it after midday already?'

'So my stomach tells me.'

An unlikely *femme fatale* in combat boots and pigtails pulled herself out of a deep beanbag and sauntered his way. She held out a hand and followed through with a nubile body until she was all but bodily against him.

'Sandra Klein,' she said. And all he could think was; girls like her get younger every year.

'Tom Campbell,' he said. 'Pleased to meet you.'

'Sorry. I should have introduced you,' Maggie blustered, her grey eyes bright, her cheeks flushed. Too much red wine? Or had he walked in on something she'd rather he hadn't?

'Tom, this is Sandra. She's a cartoonist.'

'Anything I might have seen in the funny papers?' he asked.

'Hardly,' Sandra huffed, affronted with him, which he had kind of hoped would happen, and slumping back down into her beanbag. Was it leather?

'She has her own comic. It's huge in the feminist fiction market,' Maggie explained, her tone hushed, warning him that she of the suggestive eyes might claw his eyes out with her black painted fingernails if he wasn't careful. 'Each of these talented women is a member of the fertile Sorrento artists' community. Not one of them paints beach huts.'

That was code just for him, to warn him they were serious women. Tom's cheek twitched.

'Though we four like to think ourselves a band apart,' said an older woman with riotous blonde curls, clothes better suited to a woman double her weight and eyes that seemed to see into his soul.

'You're Ashleigh Caruthers,' Tom blurted out, as if she wouldn't know who she was. *And the face in Maggie's Archibald Prize-winning portrait,* he managed to hold back. 'An old colleague of mine in Sydney is a big fan of your sculptures. He has a couple of your Tragedy series. They're wonderful.'

'Aren't they just?' Ashleigh returned. She lifted herself from her dainty chair just long enough to shake his hand before drifting back down.

'And this is Freya,' Maggie said, pointing to the woman with short red hair and pursed lips. 'The big red pot in the back doorway is one of hers. And you've likely seen her pottery in homeware stores in town.'

Tom smiled politely, not even trying to pretend that he had ever shopped in any homeware stores in town, much less noticed the pottery.

After silence reigned for a good five seconds, Freya rolled her eyes and pushed herself off her neatly folded picnic blanket, picked it up by one corner and threw it out on to the floor until it made a neat large square. 'I'll get lunch.'

'Right,' Maggie said. 'Tom, you will join us, I hope.'

Tom glanced to the kitchen, where the scent of sun-dried tomatoes and eggplant wafted on the air. But, as much as her words were telling him to stay, her eyes were begging him to leave. Besides which, he wasn't entirely sure he would survive a lunch in the company of this merry coven.

'Nah,' he said. 'I was just planning a five-minute break as is. Too much needs to be done. I'll just grab my pasta from your fridge and head back. Thanks, anyway.'

Her shoulders dropped and her throat worked and it was as good a thank you as he was going to get. He waited for Freya to depart the kitchen before he entered, grabbed his

Tupperware container from the fridge, borrowed a fork from the cutlery drawer and slipped outside with a quick, 'Nice to meet you ladies. Take care.'

It was nearly three hours later when Tom heard the sounds of loud laughing female voices spilling out the front door of the house.

'Give the girls a kiss from me,' Maggie said, after jogging back from the mailbox.

Freya gave her a hug so long he thought she might not let go. 'Shall do.'

'And remember, you must find out if your new friend is a Jack of *all* trades, okay?' Sandra asked.

Tom bit his lip to stop himself from laughing and hunkered down behind the cab of his Ute. Freya shushed Sandra and, though Tom strained to hear her response, Maggie's following words were regrettably muffled.

'Come on, girls,' Ashleigh called out. 'Our chariot awaits.' The three women waved, yelled their goodbyes and tumbled into a waiting taxi.

After they had driven away, Maggie turned and looked straight at him. Tom stopped retying the ropes on the bed of his truck and simply looked back.

Her hands shot into the back pockets of her jeans and she rolled up on to her toes, as though she was about to head down the hill to join him. But something held her back.

He gave her a small wave, she nodded back and then she ducked inside at speed. And for the rest of the afternoon Tom had to remind himself he was there for a job, not to head in for a coffee and a chat and to test if he was in fact the reason behind that new resident blush in Maggie Bryce's cheeks.

CHAPTER FIVE

EIGHT o'clock Friday night rolled around and Maggie wasn't on her usual spot on the drop cloth.

Tom sauntered over to the enclosed stairwell, which must have led up to who knew what. Huge bedrooms with high ceilings, or cramped and aching for a renovation? An attic room or two with fabulous canted roofs and quaint picture windows? Maybe one day she'd let him see them. And maybe one day he'd tell her why he was so interested. He sneaked a look upwards, but all he could see was hazy darkness.

Tom moved to wait for her by The Big Blue, even though each day it had been darker by the time he made it home. He was constantly playing catch up on the job as the chats by Maggie's painting every morning and their shared lunches got longer each day.

Even so, he couldn't seem to find the opportunity to ask her out, even with his brilliant *Nolan in the bedroom* line raring to go. He wasn't blind to the idea that maybe it was that very challenge that had him so gung-ho. Either way, so far all he'd managed was 'I like your painting.' *Nice one, Romeo*.

Tom whistled under his breath as he sauntered over to her corner and stepped over the curled edge of the paint-splattered cloth. Up close, the scent of paint was overwhelming, especially without Maggie's signature perfume to negate it.

He stared hard at The Big Blue, looking to find a similarity to the ocean view out the window, when suddenly, clear as day, he saw a face looking back at him from the canvas.

It gave him such a fright he backed up, startled. But the moment he blinked the image was gone. The painting was once again nothing more mysterious than blue smears. He stepped off the drop cloth, rubbing at his eyes. It had been a long week.

The sound of bare feet shuffling against wood announced Maggie's arrival through the front door. She flicked through a small stack of unopened mail, then threw the lot on to the bench at the front door.

'Maggie, are you sure this painting of ours is a landscape?' he asked when she joined him on her drop cloth.

'Nah,' she said. 'It's a still life of blue apples.'

'Smart arse,' he said under his breath. 'The thing is, I was sure I just saw a face in there.'

'A face,' she repeated, her surprised gaze skittering to the painting.

'Yeah.' He waved his hand over the canvas, but even he couldn't see it any more. 'Or maybe I'm going silently mad out there in your crazy old garden.'

'Why do you think I hired someone else to clear it?' she said, deadpan, as she rubbed at her neck, long thin fingers massaging deep into the tendons along the tops of her shoulders.

'Are you okay?' he asked, his attention diverted.

'Hmm,' she groaned. In the gloomy evening light her pupils filled her large eyes and sent his imagination on a trip and a half. 'Sorry, what?'

'Your neck,' he said, reaching out to her and then letting his hand drop away when her faraway gaze flickered and focused, pinning him to the spot, daring him to even think about walking one more step closer.

'What about it?' she asked, her hand still kneading her shoulder.

And Tom laughed. Out loud. No wonder he'd never worked up the nerve to ask her out; he had simply never met anyone who was as much hard work. 'You haven't stopped fussing with it since you came in.'

'I'm fine.' Maggie's hand dropped, but she couldn't hide her wince as she stopped giving it the attention that it needed.

'Of course you are.' Tom wondered what her skin would feel like beneath his hands. Would it be cool like her eyes? Or fiery like her impertinent mouth? From those few moments he'd come close enough to guess, he had the distinct feeling her skin would naturally be as warm as if she had spent half an hour basking in the sun.

In a huff Maggie turned away to stare at her painting some more, unwittingly giving Tom a perfect view of the back of her neck. Her vertebrae stuck out in a neat vertical row and fine blonde hairs whirled in tufts at the base of her chaotic ponytail. Her skin was the colour of diluted honey. Delicate. Too frail for his workman's hands.

Tom rubbed his hands together, easing away the prickling as flashes of memory of times he'd been praised on his use of those very hands skidded and tripped behind his eyes. But they soon gurgled away down a sinkhole of past reminiscences, as though he needed the room for new memories. Memories of a future in which Maggie Bryce closed her eyes, let her head roll forward until her messy ponytail slid over her shoulder, as she begged him to make her feel all better.

Taking in her furrowed brow and tight fists and earnest stare, he found the sudden need to swallow. What was he thinking? There was not one thing about the woman that said fling material. But a fling was all he could offer. No more. Never more. Not after what it had taken for him to get back on to his feet after losing Tess. So if that was all obvious, why was he expending so much energy reminding himself?

He took the one step back that left Maggie Bryce on her drop cloth island while he moved to the ocean of unpolished wood floor.

'Right,' Tom said, his voice thick. He coughed behind a tightly closed fist. 'Anyway, I came to tell you I was done for the day, so I'm heading off.'

'Okay.' But she half turned, pinning him down with that sharp grey stare, and Tom's feet stayed right where they were. 'Or you could stay for a beer.'

Maybe he wanted to find out if the beer was for real; he would have been surprised if she even had milk and bread in the fridge. Or maybe it was the idea of beer itself that had him in such a lather, considering the sweat running down his spine. Or maybe it was the hesitation in her eyes and the imagined warmth of her skin beneath his hands.

Whatever the reason, he found himself saying, 'Sure. A beer sounds great.'

'Why don't you head outside where it's cooler and I'll bring them out in a sec?'

Tom headed out to the balcony and Maggie moved into the kitchen, glad for the reprieve. Had it been getting hot in there, or was that just her? The hair at the base of her neck was stuck to her skin and all her hairs on her arms stood on end as though seeking out a cooling breeze.

She stuck her head in the fridge, savouring the cool air, and found the beer behind a whole bunch of exotic groceries she'd ordered the previous afternoon when she'd received a desperately needed letter from her bank to say some royalties had arrived in her bank account from a British calendar in which a couple of her paintings had appeared.

The money was enough to cover Belvedere's mortgage payments, so maybe she should have transferred the lot straight away and given herself another month's reprieve. But what good could another month of the same do?

Of all the noise and bluster she'd had to sit through with the Wednesday girls, one thing Freya had said *had* hit home; she was meant to be connecting with herself. The money in her bank account was a sign; the time had come to stop *marking* time. The time had come to break free from old habits.

It was like Sandra and her French cigarettes. Freya and her gourmet tastes. Ashleigh and the multitudinous textures she chose to wear against her skin. These experiential effusions all helped make them the artists and the people they were.

Well, in all twenty-nine years of her life, Maggie had never tasted beer. Moving in art circles, her bent had run to wine or late night Smirnoff. If she was going to start slaying old habits, that had seemed a painless one to start with. And Tom seemed like a beer kind of guy, so it really would have been a waste not to invite him to experience it with her. Right?

She grabbed a couple of designer bottles from the back of the fridge and then snapped the lids off using the heel of her hand and the edge of her bench like she had seen in some movie, and it worked! How was that for a new experience? The fact that she'd forgotten to buy a bottle-top opener was beside the point.

Through the kitchen window she saw Tom leaning on the balustrade of the white wooden balcony, resting his forearms along the splintered wood, no doubt surveying the huge amount of work he still had to do to get her mess of a backyard cleared.

He filled much of that view himself, he was so tall. Broad. Solid. And just plain magnificent.

Funny, but Maggie usually leaned towards finer men. Lean. Elegant. Suits and ties. Men like her dad—an executive who travelled a lot and then one day simply hadn't come home. But that hadn't stopped her from turning into the arms of men like that all her life. Men who looked the part, and said all the right things, and let her down in the end. Of all bad habits, *that* was the one she was most determined to break.

Maggie grabbed the beers with one hand and a bag of salt and vinegar crisps with the other and headed out to join her big, strong, straightforward, what-you-see-is-what-you-get handyman for a sunset drink.

'Here you go,' Maggie said, heralding her barefooted arrival so as not to startle him. He really had seemed so far away.

He turned, giving her an appreciative smile, a crooked, hazel-eyed smile that she felt deep in her belly. But that was not why she had invited him to stay. She needed a beer buddy and he'd been working hard, and he deserved some proper thanks.

He took the beer, his fingers sliding momentarily against hers as he slipped the condensation loaded bottle from her grasp.

Maggie's knees felt a little wobbly all of a sudden, so she sat in a rickety wrought iron chair and tossed the packet of crisps on to the matching mosaic table that she'd found in the backyard when she'd first moved into the house.

In fact almost every piece of furniture in the place was a found object. All bar her king-sized bed, which she had ordered from Melbourne—new, huge and ridiculously luxurious, with the most expensive white Egyptian cotton sheets from her favourite shop on Chapel Street.

She'd hoped it might help her get a good night's sleep. But so far, no deal. Maybe if she bought that second-hand stereo and a few CDs it might help her relax enough to sleep a full night. Tom said he knew which CD had that INXS song that had been playing when they'd sat together on the back of his truck. She wouldn't mind owning that one for a start.

The man in question leant his backside against the railing, the warmth of the setting sun gathering in his hair highlighting streaks of bronze amidst the dark waves. He took a swig of the beer. A great manly swig—the column of his tanned throat working overtime to down the bubbly liquid. Then he lowered his head, lowered the beer and lowered his hazel eyes to hers. And his crooked smile and her tummy twitches were back with a vengeance.

'That hit the spot,' he said. 'Thanks.'

She took her own ladylike sip.

'Interesting bunch of friends you had over the other day,' Tom said.

Maggie hid behind her right hand as she swallowed, the unfamiliar bubbles burning in her throat. 'I hope they didn't give you too much of a hard time.'

'Hardly. They were very polite.'

'Them? Never. Politeness is only a mask for what people really want to say, and those girls don't hold back.'

Tom blinked. And it hit Maggie how polite the two of them had become since that day. She remembered ripples beneath the brief hellos, even lengthier goodbyes. The pleases and thank yous galore over their shared lunches…

'I don't think the redhead liked me all that much,' Tom said, saving her from her daunting thoughts. 'Did I once cut her off in traffic?'

'Doubtful. Freya is ferociously overprotective of all of us,' Maggie said, feeling the need to over-explain to show that she wasn't holding *anything* important back. 'Hence the vibes you no doubt felt pummelling you the minute you invaded her inner sanctum of womanly placation. Don't take it personally.'

Tom nodded. 'I won't. It was a thrill to meet Ashleigh Caruthers. I had no idea she lived out here.'

'Ashleigh's the reason I bought out here in the first place.'

'She helped you find this place?' he asked, motioning with his bottle to the dark house behind them.

'Nope. This great white elephant is all my own foolishness. When I decided to buy a holiday home in Portsea a couple of years ago, it was a knee-jerk reaction to a situation I was going through at home, so it was a definite spur of the moment thing. It was the first house the estate agent offered and I took it sight unseen.'

'Are you always that spontaneous?'

She shrugged. 'I have my moments. Funnily enough, buying this place and then moving here were two of the more conspicuous ones.'

'Hmm. I'd hoped you might have an impetuous streak.'

Hoped? Maggie repeated inside her head. *Surely he meant to say 'imagined'.*

'Now, tell me more about Sandra,' he said. He raised one eyebrow suggestively and Maggie frowned and shuffled lower in her seat.

'Sandra is far too young for you,' she said, concentrating on her beer.

When Tom stopped laughing he continued to grin down at her. 'She's seems plenty old enough to make such decisions on her own. So how old do you think that makes me?'

Maggie tilted her head and took the opportunity to openly

look at his face. She'd been invited to, after all. Square jaw. Mouth permanently on the verge of a smile. Straight nose that had never seen the back end of a fight. Scruffy dark hair, with a boyish fringe that made him seem younger than he likely was.

And bold hazel eyes luminous with mirth. Mirth and a fierce intelligence. Intelligence that spoke of experience, and vitality, and even self-deprecation that made Maggie wonder if this seemingly easygoing guy had known times when not everything had gone his way.

Simply put, the guy had character radiating from his pores. Man of the earth character. Nothing manicured or elegant about him. She wondered briefly if he had ever even owned a suit and tie.

'If I say I think you're nearer forty,' she said, 'you'll likely throw that beer in my face. And if I say you're closer to my twenty-nine I'm certain you'll kiss my feet. Somewhere in between is as close as I am willing to guess.'

'Somewhere in between is pretty close.' His eyes glittered. 'But no fear, Maggie, I would never let go of a good beer in such a fashion.'

He tipped said beer her way in salute before taking another swig, and leaving her with the unspoken impression that he might yet still find it in him to kiss her feet. If she'd thought her seat uncomfortable before, she'd had no idea.

'Did I choose a good beer?' Maggie asked, deliberately changing the subject. She slithered lower in her chair and let her legs stick out straight in front of her, crossed at the ankles.

Tom pushed away from the back railing and came to sit in a chair beside hers. His big frame dwarfed the small seat and his long legs stretched out so that their feet almost touched.

'I'm enjoying every second of it,' he said, smiling over the top of his half-empty bottle. He was teasing. She felt it skidding and sliding across her nerves and along the back of her neck, before settling in a swirling mass in her tummy.

'Really?' she asked, taking a mouthful of confidence-inducing amber bubbles. 'Because I'm beginning to wonder if underneath the grease and dust and stubble, you're actually a merlot man at heart.'

Again that bark of loud, confident laughter sparked against her, bringing an indulgent smile to her own face.

Truth was, she didn't really think he was any such thing. In fact she quite liked the fact that he was a beer and sweat and suntan man. Especially since, for the first time since she had arrived in Portsea, she found herself enjoying acting the part of a beer and sweat and suntan girl.

'And what on earth is a merlot man?' Tom asked.

She kicked out with her foot and pointed at his denim-clad calf, before sliding it down to nudge against his boot. 'A man who wears Diesel jeans and two-hundred-dollar Doc Martens to weed a garden.'

For a brief second she thought she saw his cheeks grow pink beneath his stubble.

But she knew better than anyone that clothes rarely made the man. A guy in a beautiful suit could be the biggest villain on the planet. And with the money she could make selling just one portrait, she could afford to wear Ferragamo top to toe and not much care about paint splatters.

'A merlot man is someone who likes the finer things in life,' she continued now she had him on the ropes. 'A good wine. Lobster and caviare as opposed to fish and chips at The Sorrento Sea Captain. And, since you love The Big Blue so very much, we've already established you know how to appreciate a fine piece of art.'

The laughter in his eyes subsided as his gaze travelled the

length of her, from the top of her messy head to the tips of her dirty feet. There was no doubt that the piece of art he was appraising in that moment was her.

But when he looked her in the eye, his gaze was lazy and teasing. 'Naaah,' he drawled. 'I could go a newspaper filled with hot chips any day, any time.'

Maggie laughed. Just as she'd hoped.

No, not *hoped*. And why was the word *hoped* being bandied about so much tonight? It was just as she'd *expected*. Until he added, 'Though it has been some time since I've tasted lobster.'

Maggie took another sip of beer and decided to leave that statement alone. 'So what are you going to do since your kindly boss has given you the weekend off?'

'Fish.'

'Like in a boat?'

'Perhaps. Or off the Rye Pier. This time of year you can catch calamari by the bucket-load.'

'And then what?'

'Then I'll fish some more. And if I actually catch anything, and if the fish are big enough and old enough and ugly enough, I'll clean them, de-bone them, cook them over an open fire and eat them. Who needs The Sorrento Sea Captain when you've got the ocean blue?'

'I meant what else will you do besides fish? There's a whole big bright weekend ahead of you with no need for chainsaws or heavy labour.'

'What do you do when you're not painting?' he asked.

That shut her up quick smart. For the truth was since she'd come here she didn't do much. Back in Melbourne she visited galleries, went to parties, did interviews, taught classes, went shopping, made friends. Here she bit her fingernails, paced, drank too much coffee and took unnecessary drives around town to get herself out of the house. But she always returned to her work. It had become a compulsion, as if whatever was inside her had to come out on to the canvas. If only she had a clue what she was trying to say.

Tom finished his beer and placed the bottle carefully on the wobbly mosaic table then looked out at the ripe orange sky.

'So we've decided I left behind my merlot tastes in Sydney,' he said. 'How is your life most different since you left Melbourne?'

Maggie swirled her beer, transfixed by the rising bubbles. 'Oh, it's different, all right. This is the first time I have lived on my own.'

'Ever?' Tom asked.

'Yep. My dad walked out on us really suddenly when I was sixteen. Within the week, in a fit of teenage angst, I'd moved in with my then boyfriend's family. No big surprise that lasted all of a fortnight. Nevertheless I've lived with someone in some capacity or another ever since.'

'And now you're free to come and go as you please. With whomever you please. Answering to no one. This place has its advantages, don't you think?'

She shot Tom a quick look but he was still looking out into the growing darkness. 'I guess,' she said. 'But I miss the feeling that there aren't enough hours in the day. Time here is like the horizon staring back at me from my lounge room windows—it seems to go on for ever.'

'All that unwritten future,' he said, summing it up perfectly.

'It makes me nervous,' she admitted.

'It makes me feel right at home,' he said. 'Nothing ever turns out how you expect it to in life. Ever. So I've learnt not to expect anything. That way you can only be pleasantly surprised.'

'And that works for you?' she asked.

'That works for me.'

Tom leant back and crossed his arms behind his head so that Maggie had a fabulous view of more manly muscles than she had probably seen in a lifetime of knowing suit and tie men. She really was glad this man had never worked behind a desk.

'Though when I first lived alone I admit I did miss the constant company,' he said, but he kept his gaze on the sunset.

'I can't complain there, really,' Maggie said. 'I have the girls at least once a week, even though they are barking mad. I have Smiley. And the weekly grocery delivery guy from Rye, though he can't string more than two words together around me. And, well, I now have you.'

He finally turned at that. Maggie had known he would, but whether buoyed by half a bottle of beer, or the tranquil half-darkness, or the relaxing lull of conversation, she'd said it anyway.

She'd grown accustomed to having him around. And at the end of the next week she hoped he wouldn't disappear from her life altogether. Maybe they could—what? Be friends? Go fishing? He'd mentioned bowling once.

For once Tom's eyes weren't overflowing with charm and laughter; they were filled instead with unfathomable depth and shadows. And it did worse things to her equilibrium than usual. Who was she kidding? The last thing she had on her mind when she'd said those words was bowling.

She uncrossed her feet and cleared her throat, the international sign for *this has been fun but maybe we should call it a night*. But Tom reached over and opened the packet of crisps. He held out the bag to her.

'Want some?' he asked.

And it didn't take a genius to figure he wasn't talking

about the crisps. But she could hardly say no. She was the one who'd supplied them in the first place. She settled back into the chair, took a handful of crisps and gave him an ambiguous smile.

'So, Mr Handyman, here's a question for you,' she said, trying to act nonchalant, as though a new level of tension hadn't suddenly come to settle on the night. 'Did I make the most stupid decision of my life buying this old house on a whim?'

She found she really wanted to know. For the first time since she had moved into the huge empty house, she wanted to know what might one day be done to fix it up, to make it beautiful again, desirable. She wanted to see it through Tom's eyes.

'They say real estate is the best investment a person can make,' he said. 'If something ever happened to the house, at the very least you'll always have a patch of land on to which you can pitch a tent.'

Maggie's heart wrenched unexpectedly at the thought of something happening to Belvedere. She pressed her bare toes into the splintered deck as though holding on a little bit tighter than she had been before that moment.

'There's a peeling piece of wallpaper in my bedroom upstairs,' she said. 'And though from day one I have been itching to peel it away, to see what's hiding beneath, I'm kind of scared it would turn out to be a load-bearing strip and the whole house would collapse around me.'

Tom laughed. Then, deciding that her original question had been on the level, he looked through the open back door, his keen eyes taking in the warped wooden floor and the flaky ceiling paint.

She followed his gaze to see the messy drop cloth, the lack of furniture and the fact that she could still throw all her possessions in the back of her Jeep and be gone from the place in an hour and there would be no evidence she had even ever been there.

It hit her like a sucker punch to the stomach. How had she imagined she was doing right by herself, living like that, just to keep a roof over her head? To prove to people who probably couldn't care less that she could manage on her own? She thought of the fridge full of exotic groceries and felt way more proud of that decision than the majority she'd made over the past six months.

She looked back at Tom to find him no longer looking at her house with a handyman's eye. He was watching her. 'So what do you think?' she asked, her throat dry. 'What should I do?'

'I think,' he said, taking his time with each word, 'it's fine the way it is.'

Maggie laughed out loud and was surprised by the harsh sound. 'But it's a dump. On that recommendation I would guess that you were booted out of the renovation industry!'

'It's not a dump, Maggie; it's unique and utterly charming. There are no wholesale changes needed. It just needs a little tender love and care.'

Tom's eyes softened, crinkles fanned out, making him look as though he was smiling, though there really wasn't any reason for him to be. Then his long strong arm slowly lowered from its place behind his head and he ran a finger across her forehead and tucked a stray wisp of hair behind her ear.

Maggie couldn't even hope to disguise the sigh that escaped her lips at his small sign of tenderness. A human touch. A man's touch. Tom's touch. It was all she could do not to lean into his hand and purr.

But then, before she was able to fully enjoy it, it was gone. Tom was moving away from her, standing, stretching his arms over his head, the manly creak and crack of joints jolting her out of her shameful reverie. She let out a long wavering breath and stood on wobbly legs.

'It's dark,' Tom said. 'I ought to head off.'

He was right. Some time while they had been talking the sun had set, the rising moon casting very little glow on the ocean.

He turned back to her, his words telling her he was ready to leave, but his eyes and his aura and his tensely bunched muscles telling her the exact opposite.

'Thanks for the beer,' he said.

'Any time,' she returned, her voice a throaty whisper.

He was waiting for her to say goodbye. But she couldn't. She could barely feel her feet, much less order them to move out of his way. The feelings churning inside her were tumbling in too fast, too unexpectedly. She wasn't even sure what he wanted from her, much less what she wanted from him—

Tom gave in first. He took two bold steps to stand before her, toe to toe. He looked down into her eyes—eyes, she knew, which were wide with disbelief and desire. He lifted a gentle hand, resting the backs of his knuckles against her cheek, and suddenly she couldn't remember how to breathe.

More to keep her balance than out of any form of invitation, Maggie lifted a hand to rest against his chest. She felt a tremble shudder through Tom's rock-solid body and only then did she finally recognise the depth of the attraction that had been simmering between them for days.

It had crept up on her, lacing surreptitiously through the back recesses of her mind until the feeling was woven so tight she had the horrible sense she would never be able to fully unravel it.

She'd counted on herself being more careful. More resilient. More uncompromising. After what she'd been through in the last couple of years, that should have been a given.

What she hadn't counted on was Tom Campbell walking through her door…

'Nobody in their right mind ought to go around smelling as good as you do, Maggie Bryce,' Tom said.

He lowered his head and Maggie half-panicked and half-hoped he was about to kiss her, but he changed direction at the last moment and leaned in to her neck and inhaled a long luxurious breath. She tilted her head to give him better access.

'You were right about my merlot tastes,' he murmured. 'I am rendered hopeless in the presence of a fine perfume.'

'You are?' she asked, now not much caring what he said any more, so long as he kept saying it while breathing against her throat.

'Mmm,' he said, giving over to her wish.

'I've always worn it,' she babbled, 'to cover the smell of the paint. No matter how many showers I take, or how vigorously I wash my hands, it never seems to leave.'

'Just one more reason to love that crazy blue painting of yours,' he said.

Maggie felt herself smiling. Not just with her mouth and her cheeks, but her whole body. She felt herself warming and tingling and opening to him with every passing second.

But she shouldn't be doing this, feeling this. She wasn't ready. Or willing. Or able. Mentally. Emotionally. Morally…

Her neck felt cold and she realised he had pulled away. Her eyelids fluttered open to find him looking down at her. His hot hazel eyes were dark in the low light, but there was absolutely no doubt as to what was about to happen. They were going to kiss and it was going to be bone-melting. Earth-shattering. Like nothing she had ever experienced in her life before.

And though in that moment she wanted it more than she remembered wanting anything, her conscience and her memory and her reason gave her a much-needed slap to the face. So hard she actually flinched.

'Tom,' she whispered, his name all but lodging in her tight throat.

'Yes, Maggie,' he drawled, his deep voice reverberating so close to her lips. 'Tell me what you want.'

'I want you to wait.'

The hand against his chest pressed him away. Barely. Half-heartedly. But it was enough for his momentum to cease.

'What's wrong?' he asked, looking so deep inside her she almost forgot what she had been about to say. Almost.

But the worst mistake she could possibly make was to break an old bad habit only by creating a brand-new one.

'Tom, I can't. I just can't.'

'And why's that?'

'Because…I'm married.'

CHAPTER SIX

TOM burst out laughing. It was hardly the reaction either of
them would have expected at the announcement of Maggie's
news. But it was either that or kick something.

'Did you just say that you are married?' he asked.

She nodded, a wisp of biscuit-blonde hair escaping her
messy ponytail and hanging forlornly along the curve of her
cheek. 'It wasn't a joke.'

He knew it wasn't a joke. That was not why he'd laughed.
He'd laughed because there he was, ready to make the first
move, to throw caution to the wind, to disregard his usual
modus operandi of keeping relationships on a tight leash, and
she had to go and say—*that.*

Maggie blinked up at him, those shining silver eyes
swirling with a heady mix of self-reproach and desire, and
Tom was shocked to find how much he still wanted to ignore
one and give in to the other, despite her recent revelation.
She had felt so good melting against him—delicate and
warm and willowy and beautiful, like the tragic heroine in
some silent movie.

But he was the tragic one. He should have seen it coming—
with her abandoned garden, her insomnia, her missing muse
and that delicate sadness cloaking her, the way she gravitated

towards him even as she kept him at arm's distance. She wore her guilt like a badge of honour on her chest.

The side-splitting thing was, he'd seen the signs yet that was *why* he'd kept on moving in—because the knight in shining armour inside him had thought he'd found his ultimate damsel in distress.

He turned his back on her and ran a hand through his hair. Hard. Tugging the roots as he went. Since he didn't have a bucket of ice water at hand it was the best he could do.

'So where is this elusive husband of yours?' he asked when she remained silent, feeling suddenly angry at her for making him do all the work.

'Carl still lives in Melbourne.'

Carl. Carl still lived in Melbourne, did he?

Tom turned back to find her pink-cheeked, hair a tumble and legs braced shoulder-width apart. Her hands were shaking. Violently. And it took all of his strength not to go to her and haul her into his arms until the shaking stopped.

Now, what the hell was *that* about? He'd always liked women who were confident. Bold. Forward, even. Those who made the first move and never shed a tear when the time came to move on. Not fragile women with chaotic hair and dirty feet and temperaments so stubborn that they would rather go six months without a couch than admit that they weren't coping.

'Your husband is in Melbourne,' he repeated. 'I assume he's been there all the time you've been here.'

She nodded.

'And is this some sort of *open* marriage? He has his floozies in the city, while you like yours beachcombed?' he said and her head jolted back as though she had been slapped.

Tom ground his teeth. Spitting venom wasn't going to help the situation, not if they were going to come out the other side and still be able to look one another in the eye. When everything was said and done, neither of them had done anything worse than finally admit the fact that until about thirty seconds before they had both been hugely in-like with one another.

He took a step back towards her, ready to say so, but her hands moved, just enough to halt him in his tracks.

'He has just the one floozy in the city,' she said, her voice as cold as chipped ice. 'That I'm aware of.'

Tom's lungs pressed hard against his ribs as he sucked in a great mouthful of oxygen. He was glad Carl was in Melbourne and not in the next room, or in that moment Carl might have been in a lick of trouble.

'Carl is an entertainment lawyer,' Maggie continued. 'He *was* my lawyer. And it turns out he has been...seeing another lawyer from his firm for over two years.'

She didn't blink. Not once. But he could see the turmoil behind the glassy stare. The aloofness was a defence mechanism. He could see that now. Rather than sending him bolting out the door once and for all, it only made the impulse to protect her more tangible.

'She represents footballers, mainly.' She shook her head, as though somehow that only made it worse. 'She is currently pregnant with his child. And the day I left Melbourne to move here I served him with divorce papers.'

Maggie leant on to the railing, as though she couldn't trust her own strength to keep her upright any more. Her hands gripped the balustrade as he had seen her grip the steering wheel of her Jeep, as though needing the support to keep herself upright. Tom's fists clenched so hard at his sides that his fingers began to feel nerveless.

'So what am I? Some sort of payback?' he asked. But he had

to know. Before they could go on, forward or backward, he had to know what was going on in that complicated head of hers.

'No,' she said, closing her eyes and shaking her head. 'I haven't seen Carl in six months. I've only talked to him through our lawyers since the day I left. So he has no reason to be hurt by your presence.'

Touché. But it wasn't what *he* thought that was important. It was what she thought. She was the wronged party in her relationship with her husband. Who knew what she would do to make herself no longer feel like the victim? Or *who* she would do.

Either way, now was not the time to put that question to the test. It was still too raw, even though every desire to kiss her had now fled his body. Okay, not every desire, but his head now had the upper hand. Tom figured his best option was to give both of them some space. Some distance and a cold shower. He was downright grateful the weekend stretched out before them.

'I think I should go, Maggie.'

'Probably a good idea.'

He made a move to leave, but he knew he'd only kick himself all weekend if he left her feeling guilty. He'd made the first move and she'd put a stop to it. Bar being beautiful and fascinating, she'd done nothing wrong.

'You did the right thing telling me about Carl.'

It took longer than he would have liked for her to nod. Then, without another word, he ran down the last of the steps and to his truck.

He could only hope his weekend would not now be shot through by images of that neck, those eyes and that scent. Of the package that was Maggie Bryce. Painter. Fighter.

And married woman.

* * *

For Maggie, Saturday was a complete bust.

The Big Blue was still big, still blue and she could barely concentrate, much less begin to decipher what it was she was meant to be painting. She threw her dry paintbrush into a jar of clean water and jogged upstairs to the fourth floor master bedroom.

The white sheets and light blanket were twisted and hanging off the end of the bed in tumbled abandon, evidence of an interrupted night's sleep. Two pillows were scrunched together on one side of the bed. Her side. Where she had slept alone. Where she'd been sleeping alone for six months.

Heck, if she was honest with herself, she'd been sleeping alone for years. Even on those few nights in which Carl had fallen into bed before two in the morning, he may as well have been sleeping in another room for all the affection he'd shown towards her. But still she'd hung on, hoping this time she could love a man enough to keep him from abandoning her.

She ignored the mess and headed into the shower. Nothing like water to get her thoughts in order. Though so far the six months of staring at the curved horizon of Port Phillip Bay hadn't produced any wonders, but it was doing its job just fine. The lack of progress was her fault, her woolly-headedness, her too tight grip, her craving for distractions.

Maggie grabbed a loofah and a cake of cinnamon scented soap and lathered herself vigorously from head to toe in an effort to dismiss the biggest distraction of all.

Tom.

Was he out there somewhere, fishing, and thinking awful things about her? She couldn't blame him if he was, for she wasn't entirely blameless in allowing him to think he'd had a chance with her. He *had* had a chance.

She scrubbed her hair clean, running her fingernails ferociously over her scalp.

One thing for sure—she couldn't stand to be cooped up in the house any more. The thought of standing in the one corner of the one room and looking at that one bloody painting all afternoon made her itch. She had to get out. To get her mind off…things. And the best way she knew how to do that? Shopping. Maggie was going to buy herself a stereo. And on her travels she'd keep clear of the Rye Pier, just in case.

Dressed in neat jeans, a pretty three-quarter-sleeved cardigan she'd found at the back of her wardrobe and flat canvas shoes that felt strange on feet which had been bare for so long, she drove out of her bumpy front drive, overhanging branches scratching at the roof of her Jeep, then down the lightly graded Portsea Hill and into Sorrento, grabbing the last angled parking space overlooking the beach.

Sorrento was busy with Melbourne families in town for the weekend to get a taste of the summer that was buzzing on the horizon. She would loathe missing summer in the seaside town, especially after she had made it through the long, cold, lonely winter.

Shoving that thought aside, Maggie headed into the picturesque town, where she spent the afternoon browsing through the quaint local shops, running her hands over piles of Freya's beautiful pots, falling madly in love at first sight with a lounge suite the colour of her favourite coffee, which thankfully was on hold for somebody else so she could put it out of her mind.

Finally she found an electronics shop that stocked mainly digital cameras and paraphernalia to cater to the tourist trade. But up the back it had a small section of TVs and stereos. They cost more than she'd expected. And she hesitated.

Maggie *hated* that she hesitated. It had been such a fun afternoon until she hesitated. Why did she have to do that all the time? Second guess herself? Her choices? Her decisions? Her desires? Especially now, as a particular gentleman had pointed out to her, when living alone she answered to no one bar herself.

And then the back of her neck prickled as she remembered something else Tom had said: *Nothing ever turns out how you expect it to in life. Ever. So I've learnt not to expect anything.*

She'd thought it a sad kind of statement at the time. But as she stood staring at the stereos, playing the kind of soft rock music she could imagine Tom listening to while working in the sun, she wondered if she'd been looking at it all wrong. Maybe the whole point was to stop *expecting* everything to go belly-up. Two moments of sheer spontaneity had led her to move to Portsea. And she was still standing. Maybe the key was to continue how she'd begun.

Within five minutes Maggie had bought herself a stereo. Then, in the post purchase flush, she realised she needed somewhere to put it, so she picked out a rustic mahogany entertainment unit, which would look pretty silly without a TV, so she picked out one of those as well.

An hour later, she headed down the hill, feeling a little light-headed about the amount of money she had spent. But it was a good kind of light-headed. A hopeful kind of light-headed. A raspberry in the face of her past kind of light-headed.

At the bottom of the hill she found herself standing outside The Sorrento Sea Captain, a rustic pub on the ground floor of a corner hotel, across the road from the beach. It was early evening and she'd eaten little more than her usual coffee-rich diet. The idea of fish and chips actually sounded pretty fine, in spite of the fact that she'd once accused Tom of frequenting the place against his better judgement.

She walked inside to find the place was full of senior citizens on a bus tour, and some familiar faces from her few and far between outings into town. She even received several waves, a couple of hellos and half a dozen smiles, which made her blush to her roots when she thought of how little she had done to get to know any of them.

Standing alone in the doorway, she felt as if everyone was looking at her. The hustle and bustle of the place, the sharp scraping of chairs, clinking of billiard balls and screeches of people laughing uproariously in the far bar was somewhat overwhelming considering the peace and quiet she was used to at home.

Her light-headedness began to morph into a headache. Maybe this was too much too soon; maybe she'd been kidding herself when she'd thought she could loosen up, fit in, be happy. Maybe she ought to just get back to her painting, the one place where she could be herself and no one could judge her…

'Table for one?' asked a skinny young girl, all in black, an oft washed apron, and chewing gum in the side of her mouth.

A table for one? Maggie couldn't remember the last time she had eaten out alone. If ever. Surely that was one old habit it was time to break.

'Ma'am?'

'A table for one would be fantastic,' she said, and she wasn't all that surprised when the teenager looked at her as if she was crazy to be so excited about that fact.

Tom strolled back towards his car from the old Sorrento Baths café where he'd been organising a future date to re-stain their deck.

The scent of grease and overcooked steak wafted from the restaurant on the corner. He glanced absent-mindedly inside and his feet came to an abrupt halt when he saw Maggie sitting behind a large rickety table reading a menu. She was alone, and by the deep look of concentration on her face the menu may have been written in Sanskrit.

Considering the day he'd just had—a day when even fishing off the sand at dawn, rereading a worn old Dick Francis novel in the hammock by his beach hut, jogging ten miles and playing Playstation with Alex's girls had done not a thing to relax him—he knew he ought to just keep walking.

Heck, he'd actually gone to the Sorrento Baths asking for work, trying to prepare for life beyond Maggie's garden—beyond her tempting lips, her earnest eyes, and beyond the fact that, for two decent people, they had come very, very close to cheating on her husband.

Okay, so he'd go in, be polite, say hello, make like everything was A-okay, and then leave her to her dinner. Then the next week would fly and they'd get on with their lives. Tom almost convinced himself the sudden uncomfortable churning in his stomach was hunger.

'Here goes nothing,' he said, before walking over to her table and sitting down. Maggie blinked up at him, those great grey eyes of hers all confusion for a brief second, before they brightened, turning to molten silver.

His head knew she only looked so darned happy to see him because it meant she wouldn't be sitting there alone. But his heart obviously hadn't received the memo that she was off the market as it missed a beat in response. He mentally told it to get a grip on itself.

'What are you doing here?' she asked. 'I thought you'd be out fishing.' *Which is why I braved coming into town*, her eyes said, even if her words did not. At least one of them was prudent.

'Been there, done that. Have you ordered yet?' he asked,

grabbing a spare menu from the next table. So much for saying hello and heading off. It seemed his hands and voice box had joined the rebel side along with his feet and his heart.

'Ah, no,' she said, sitting on her hands and looking sheepish. 'I've been here for about twenty minutes and I think I may have been forgotten.'

'That's because you're meant to order at the bar.'

'Oh.' Her eyes grew wide. Her cheeks grew pink.

Tom sat on his own hands to stop himself from reaching out and cupping her cheek and telling her that he wasn't such a nice guy after all and he could forget about her husband if she could.

'Then do you mind watching my handbag while I order?' she asked.

'Sure. Go ahead.'

She grabbed her wallet and slid out of the booth seat, knocking knees with him and giving him a shy smile by way of apology.

It's nothing more than an accidental knee knock! he told himself, but his skin felt a degree warmer all the same. 'And while you're there order me the crumbed fish and fries,' he said. 'Extra slice of lemon.'

'You're staying for dinner?' she asked. He'd imagined that she would find a kind way of telling him to leave, but instead he caught a flare of hope in her eyes.

What the heck did the two of them think they were playing at? There was no way Tom could leave now without finding out. He leaned back and rested an arm along the edge of the booth seat.

'Thank you. I'd love to.'

'Good,' she said, blushing even deeper. 'I'll get the same as you. Though I think I'll order my fish beer-battered.'

Beer-battered fish? Why did that just have to be another thing for Tom to like about her?

'You're living on the edge tonight, Ms Bryce,' he drawled. 'Fish and chips, dinner in town, no paint stains. I hardly know you.'

'You know me just fine,' she said. Then she half smiled, half frowned, looked as though she was about to say something, then shook her head, spun on her heel and walked away.

Tom let out his breath in a great whoosh of air as he watched her willowy form slinking between the closely stacked tables.

When she disappeared behind a pillar, he rubbed both hands over his face. Hard and fast. He should have been paying closer attention to the reasons why she was all wrong for him. It hadn't been a hard task at other times, with other women. When he'd ever felt as if he was getting too close, he'd pulled away. Simple as that. So why couldn't he simply switch it off with Maggie?

Maybe it *was* the fact that he couldn't have her that was making her that much more desirable. Hunting, gathering and survival of the fittest. The instinctive desire to be the dominant male.

Tom laughed. Out loud. While sitting all on his lonesome. Heads turned. He smiled and waved to the octogenarian Clements, who were glaring at him as though he'd sworn in church.

Since when had he become an expert in animal husbandry? Since never, that was when. Even he could see that he was getting desperate. But he'd learnt to live without the priorities that were part and parcel of a city life. He could live without merlot and lobster. And he could live without Maggie Bryce.

'Tommy Boy!'

Tom looked up to find his cousin sliding into the seat Maggie had recently vacated. 'Hey, Alex. What are you doing here?'

'On a date with Marianne.' Alex motioned over his shoulder to his long-suffering wife and the table full of daughters.

Tom waved to Marianne, who grimaced back. 'You romantic old dog, you.'

Alex grinned. 'So what's with you and Lady Bryce? Don't tell me you're on some sort of date yourselves.' Alex leaned in and whispered conspiratorially, 'She is married, you know.'

Tom laughed so loud he felt it rumble through his shoes, but this time he didn't much care who was staring at him. 'So I've recently discovered. How did you find out?'

'The Barclay sisters told me when I picked up something for Marianne at their shop a couple of days ago.'

'Of course they did. And you didn't think to pass that news on to me?'

Alex shrugged. 'I wasn't aware it was a concern.' His eyes narrowed. 'Is it? A concern?'

Tom glanced at Maggie, who was three rooms away, leaning forward and pointing to something on the menu above the cashier's head.

'She's getting divorced,' he said.

'Not good enough, Tommy Boy.'

'I know,' Tom said, the wistfulness in his voice a surprise even to him as Maggie turned, weaving her way back through the crowd, shyly smiling at anyone who caught her eye.

'Don't do anything I wouldn't do,' Alex warned, getting out of the chair.

Tom didn't get the chance to make that promise. Maggie's eyes had already zeroed in on his. She smiled. It was a half smile. A cautious smile. But still he couldn't help but smile back.

It took some kind of superhuman concentration for Tom

to remind himself why he hadn't been able to sleep a wink despite the soft slap of ocean waves cooing through his bedroom window, or catch a fish despite the perfect weather conditions, or last at his beach hut haven longer than twenty frustrating minutes.

He wanted her still. And Maggie Bryce wasn't his for the wanting.

CHAPTER SEVEN

AFTER another hour of gossiping about the locals, about Tom's poor cousin Alex and his band of merry women, and the elderly diner who thought 'handyman' was code for Lothario and wouldn't give Tom the time of day, Maggie's cheeks hurt from laughing. And from pretending that she was having fun.

Tom, in dark jeans, soft olive-coloured sweater and not a lick of sweat on him, seemed even more overwhelmingly masculine than he did bare-armed and reeking pheromones with a chainsaw in his hands. And she could no longer deny that something vital had shifted inside her last night when Tom had whispered sweet nothings in her ear—an awareness, a need, a longing.

And the longer their feet kept bumping beneath the table, sending her nerves into a permanent twitch, the more she came to realise that just saying 'no' wasn't going to be enough to shift everything back.

Finally, one moment, late in the evening, when their conversation hit a lull, Maggie couldn't stand it a second longer. 'We need to talk,' she blurted out.

The last thing she expected was for Tom to groan dramatically and lower his head until it thunked on to the table. It made her laugh. For real. But the pleasure that came from laughing only added to the tension building inside her.

Tom lifted his head and rubbed his hands up and down over his face until he looked at her from between his long fingers. 'Don't you know those are *the* four words every man dreads more than any other?'

'Apart from *what are you thinking*?' Maggie said, smiling despite herself.

Tom slowly lowered his hands and he was grinning. Her skin warmed a full degree. Dammit! The fact that she was officially married didn't mean the affection she felt for Tom was going to go away.

'To-o-o-m?' she begged, shaking the table and sounding like a whining teenager.

He nodded. Then said, 'Right. Okay. But maybe here's not the best place for it. These walls have ears.' He winked at someone over her shoulder to tell them the table was about to be freed up.

She could feel his presence all the way to the bistro's front door. She knew his hand hovered at her lower back. She knew his eyes followed her as she walked ahead of him. She could sense it all as they walked together out into the lonely moonlit street, the light sea breeze thankfully cooling her heated skin.

'We need to talk about last night,' she said the second they were out of earshot of the noisy diners.

'Hang on,' Tom said. His hovering hand landed upon her back and gave her a little forward pressure in the direction of the beach. It would only have to move about three inches to the right before he would officially have his arm around her waist. But when they hit the shrouded pathway, huge dark pine trees towering above them, covering the pathway in dead

NO POSTAGE
NECESSARY
IF MAILED
IN THE
UNITED STATES

BUSINESS REPLY MAIL
FIRST-CLASS MAIL   PERMIT NO. 717-003   BUFFALO, NY

POSTAGE WILL BE PAID BY ADDRESSEE

HARLEQUIN READER SERVICE
3010 WALDEN AVE
PO BOX 1867
BUFFALO NY 14240-9952

Do You Have the LUCKY KEY?

PLAY THE Lucky Key Game

and you can get

FREE BOOKS and FREE GIFTS!

Scratch the gold areas with a coin. Then check below to see the books and gifts you can get!

YES! I have scratched off the gold areas. Please send me the 2 FREE BOOKS and 2 FREE GIFTS for which I qualify. I understand I am under no obligation to purchase any books, as explained on the back of this card.

314 HDL EL34   114 HDL ELTT

FIRST NAME	LAST NAME

ADDRESS

APT.#	CITY

STATE/PROV.   ZIP/POSTAL CODE

www.eHarlequin.com

🗝🗝🗝🗝 2 free books plus 2 free gifts   🗝🗝🗝🗝 1 free book

🗝🗝🗝🗝 2 free books   🗝🗝🗝🗝 Try Again!

Offer limited to one per household and not valid to current Harlequin Romance® subscribers.
Your Privacy – Harlequin Books is committed to protecting your privacy. Our Privacy Policy is available online at www.eHarlequin.com or upon request from the Harlequin Reader Service. From time to time we make our lists of customers available to reputable firms who may have a product or service of interest to you. If you would prefer us not to share your name and address, please check here. ☐

DETACH AND MAIL CARD TODAY!

(H-R-06/07)

© 2002 HARLEQUIN ENTERPRISES LTD ® and ™ are trademarks owned and used by the trademark owner and/or its licensee.

brown pine needles, Tom spun her to face him and then his hand slipped away.

'*Nothing* happened last night,' he said. His expression was hooded in the low dusk light. Watchful.

'Nothing?' Maggie repeated. 'But—'

'*But*,' he said, cutting her off. He held up a hand, as though he was about to cup her face. But it stopped halfway between them, hovering like some kind of promise. 'Something *could* have happened, which I think is the point you are trying to make.'

She nodded.

'I like you, Maggie,' he said. 'I can't deny that, and I wouldn't want to. I like our chats. I like the way you tidy your hair only to make a bigger mess. I even like your terrible sandwiches because I know the care that has gone into them. And last night I would have been quite happy to have kissed you. I think that's fairly evident without us having to talk ourselves silly about it. Right?'

Maggie bit at the inside of her lip. He liked her. She knew it, but hearing him say it only made it all the more real. And immediate. And enticing. For she liked him right on back. And if he was going to continue coming to her place every day, and taking off his shirt and smiling at her and sharing his meals and jokes and saying nice things about The Big Blue, then she was fairly sure she was only going to like him more and more.

'*But* you're married,' Tom continued, 'and I'm not the kind of guy to make light of that. No matter the circumstances. So, as far as I can see, there's nothing more to talk about. I think we are both bright enough to know when we're beaten.'

He was right. The facts were the facts. And nothing was going to happen between them. Good. Excellent. Fabulous. But she itched to just ask him outright how he could run so hot and cold, how one minute he could make her feel so sure that he had wanted to kiss her until her toes curled and her lips ached and her stomach melted into a pool of heat, and the next minute simply move on. She barely managed to hold it all in.

'How about we wind down? Walk off dinner,' Tom said.

She did her best impersonation of indifference and said, 'Sure, why not?'

Tom motioned to the Sorrento Pier ahead of them, where dawdling seagulls cooed and dived for scraps on the low tide sands and the great white Queenscliff to Sorrento Ferry had just left mooring on its final trip across The Rip.

Maggie had to walk carefully so that her slippery soles didn't slide over the wide cracks between the old wooden planks of the pier. Tom reached out to take her hand in his to guide her through, but she ignored it. Instead she slipped out of her flat canvas shoes and went the rest of the way barefoot. The feel of the crusty old wood felt good beneath her feet. It grounded her.

They reached the end in silence. A week before she would have walked to the far side of the pier and given in to the tug of the city lights across the bay. But tonight she followed Tom's lead and looked back towards the bay where the sweep of the bay was dotted with the massive houses of Portsea and the familiar row of quaint and colourful beach huts.

'There's Belvedere,' Tom said, his long arm pointing off to her right.

Maggie searched the cliff tops and spotted her great white hope peeping through the masses of brambles. Her gaze skittered down the rocky cliff to find...

'There's a beach!' she cried out. It was hardly Surfers Paradise, but there was a skinny stretch of neat white sand below her home. She felt something swell inside her at the sight. Pride? Hope? Contentment?

'Can you see your place from here?' she asked.

He waved a hand towards the cliffs. 'It's out there somewhere.'

Something in the timbre of his voice made her turn to look at him. *Out there somewhere?* She realised she had no clue as to where the guy lived. In what. Or with whom. 'Where is it?' she demanded. 'Show me.'

Tom bent over to lean his forearms along the railing, his gaze far away, his chin stubborn. Maggie pushed on.

'Come on, Tom. You've spent more hours this week in my home than you likely have in your own. You could live in a caravan, under a palm tree or in some dumbfounding mansion fit for Architectural Digest as far as I know.'

'That I could,' he agreed and his cheek twitched.

'From the little you've told me about you this week, you could be married with ten kids by now,' she said.

'*I'm* not married,' he said pointedly.

'Fine,' she said, spinning back to look out over the cliffs. 'Don't tell me.'

Don't tell me? Suddenly that one question opened up a slew of others. Had he ever been married? Divorced? Did he have a girlfriend? A family? He hadn't said to her that he didn't have kids…

'Maggie,' he said, and her tense, frustrated gaze skittered to his.

'What?' she shot back.

'I thought we were meant to be winding down.' He smiled. It was a smile of pure understanding. And her tense stomach turned to liquid. 'Just relax.'

'Fine,' she whispered, before taking a deep breath, bending over to mirror Tom's attitude and letting her shoes dangle over the edge of the white wooden railing.

The sky was streaked with deep blue, bright apricot and slashes of pale grey clouds. The same colours glinted back up at her from the still waters of the bay. The heavily clumped trees on the cliffs created dark, shadowy holes in the Technicolor vista. And in the back of her mind she mixed paint colours on her palette to try to make just that perfect shade of sooty green that glowered back at her from Belvedere's backyard.

At the edge of her vision she caught sight of Tom's hands. Workman's hands. Hands that last night had trailed across her forehead and down her cheek as he had tucked a strand of hair behind her ear. She shivered as the memory took her over.

'Are you cold?' Tom asked.

Maggie shook her head. 'I'm okay.'

Nonetheless, Tom reached out and took her hands in his, rubbing warmth back into them. Her skinny hands. Her bony knuckles. Her rough, often blistered palms. But within his large, brawny, tanned, labourer's hold they felt dainty, ladylike and cherished as he ran his palms over them, around them, intertwining their fingers and then completely enclosing her hands in his.

It hit Maggie that this was the first real prolonged physical contact they'd had. Could that be right? How could she be feeling what she was feeling when they had barely even touched? She had no idea.

But what she did learn, as Tom cradled her hands so carefully in his, caressing her palms and holding her as if she was something precious, was that she wasn't alone in her disorientation. Tom was right there with her, stretching out the night just to be near her.

Maggie was suddenly hit with a wave of sensory awareness so strong she had no choice but to close her eyes and drink it in. Sea air. Salt on the tongue. Crisp, wintry aftershave.

A scent reminiscent of the vinegar that Tom had poured over his fries. And something else soft and homey. Something delectable and comforting. Paint? Wood stain?

Tom, she thought on an inner sigh.

This was all too hard. It had taken her twenty-nine years and a failed marriage to realise that her instincts about this sort of thing sucked. She *couldn't* fall into the same old trap of mistaking attention for affection; she would only be hurt in the end.

A low rumbling laugh rolled from the man beside her. 'You're not all that relaxed, are you?' he said.

'Not all that much,' she admitted. 'But I'm trying.'

'That you are,' Tom said and with a great sigh he tucked her hand in his and led her away from the railing and back down the pier towards the shore. When they reached her Jeep he let her go.

'Thanks for staying for dinner, Tom,' she said, shoving her tingling hands into the safe back pockets of her jeans. 'I had a really nice time.'

'No more jibes about the Captain, then?' he asked, his mouth kicking into that easy smile of his.

'We'll see how he digests tonight.'

'See you Monday, Maggie,' he said, backing away.

'Looking forward to it,' she admitted, and even she heard the wayward note of longing in her voice.

Tom's boot seemed to catch against something on the ground and his backward momentum ceased. Maggie's breath caught in her throat, until he lifted his foot and kept moving away.

He gave her a quick salute, then turned and headed up the hill towards—who knew where? The Hotel Sorrento, in which he kept a small suite? The shell of an abandoned car he slept in at night? A lean-to in the woods?

Maggie furiously jabbed the key into her car door with the

promise that she would wholeheartedly spend the next week finishing The Big Blue, leaving Tom to finish the job of clearing her damn brambles, and *not* reliving the moment she had watched the sun set with her hands enclosed in his.

By the time the sun had set on Monday night, Maggie had spent a whole day ignoring Tom as best she could. It wasn't all that easy when the soft strains of his stereo reminded her she wasn't alone.

The only time she'd said two words to him all day had been when she'd begged off lunch, claiming she was mid-breakthrough with The Big Blue. Tom had stood at the back steps, staring her down for way longer than she thought entirely necessary before giving in and going back outside to eat his lunch alone.

But somehow, as though through the sheer force of her will, The Big Blue had moved forward in leaps and bounds. She tipped her head to one side, twirled her paintbrush in her right hand and began to hum. Nothing in particular, just a melodious tune. For, though she might not be the greatest landscape artist in the world, this painting was sure beginning to look like...something.

'*Bright Eyes,*' Tom's deep voice said.

Maggie leapt a good inch in the air as the man at the forefront of her mind appeared from nowhere. She spun towards him with her hand on her chest and only realised that her paintbrush was wet with paint when it seeped through her T-shirt. With a muffled oath, she swiped at her shirt and tossed the brush into a jar of water and turned back to Tom.

'What did you just say?' she asked, half angry at herself for being so flustered and half angry at him for been so able to make her feel that way.

'*Bright Eyes,*' he said, coming towards her like a mirage from the dark shadows of the doorway. 'You know, the song by Art Garfunkel.'

Maggie knew it. Intimately. 'What about it?'

'You've been humming it for days. I thought I'd picked it more times than I can count, but I wasn't even close.'

He congratulated himself for another good ten seconds before he seemed to realise that she was leaning back on her workbench, gripping on to the edge for all her might.

'Maggie, are you okay?' He took a single step forward, his face creased with concern.

Maggie didn't answer. Instead she pushed herself away from the bench and turned on numb feet to face her painting. It was so obvious. Like one of those magic eye drawings where you had to look with the right distance and perspective to see the real picture beneath the dots.

'My father used to sing that song to me when I was a little girl,' Maggie said, running her fingers over the soft, dusty image of a right cheek. 'He asked me to paint him a self-portrait when I was seven so he could take it with him when he went on business trips interstate.'

Tom moved slowly up next to her, his eyes roving over The Big Blue, widening in amazement as he too saw the fine jaw, the straight nose, the sweep of straight hair and the sad cavernous eyes. 'Holy heck,' he whispered.

'I gave him another self-portrait, framed, for his fortieth birthday,' she said. 'It was a picture I still to this day think is better than my Archibald winner. But when he left for good, he left that painting behind as well. It hurt me so much I haven't painted a picture of myself since. Until now…'

'You're really in there, aren't you?'

'I really am,' she said, pulling her hand back from the

canvas to rub at her upper arms, though it did little to protect her against the wave after wave of emotion bombarding her. 'What do you think it means?'

Tom moved in closer and, reaching across, took her shaking left hand in his, drawing it to his chest. 'We've been known to do strange things in order to fight our way out from under the burden of heartache.'

She knew she ought to pull away, not allow herself to give in to the comfort of being touched by him, held by him, cared for by him. But, as though sensing she was about to move away, Tom's grip only grew tighter. So tight she felt pain. But the pain wasn't in her hand. It was in her heart. For she realised he was talking from experience.

'You moved here right after your sister died,' she remembered aloud, her voice barely above a whisper.

'That I did.'

'Why?'

He turned back to the painting, seeming to give it his whole attention again. 'When Tess died I was on the other side of the world, trying to lure a Canadian specialist back to Sydney to see her. She died holding the hand of a home nurse she'd only met three days beforehand. When I came back to our home to the knowledge that she would never be there again, the manner in which I had been living my life didn't have the same meaning any more. So I sold up, moved to the beach, and now, here I am.'

Maggie's heart twisted so severely she thought it might rupture. She didn't know what to say. That she understood why he'd run? That she understood why he expected so little of life, and especially of himself, now? If only the guy knew how great he was. She ran her thumb back and forth along his palm.

'Don't get me wrong,' he said, glancing her way. His cheek

lifted into a wry smile but his eyes were masked by the lengthening shadows in the dark room. 'Moving here was the best decision of my life.'

Just as it could be the best decision of yours, his eyes seemed to say. *If only you'd let it.*

'This place is all about new memories,' she allowed. So many weird and wonderful new memories. And now, when she'd begun to appreciate them, it felt as if they were about to slip right through her fingers. Maggie turned away from Tom's all too discerning gaze, but that only brought her face to face with herself again.

'The big question is, why now?' he said. 'Why didn't The Big Blue come out when you hooked up with…Carl?'

She heard his hesitation, and felt the tumble of emotions again shoot from his hand to hers. Though this time they were harder to pin down. Fuzzy. Confused. And far too redolent of her own emotions in that moment.

She shook her head. 'I have no idea. They never met. Though they would have been best buds. Well-heeled. Old-fashioned. Prone to mid-life crises. They could have started a club. With me as mascot.'

'They do say girls go after men like their fathers.'

'Well, *they* saw me coming a mile away.'

Tom smiled, and she was relieved to see a hint of the sparkle return. 'Don't be so hard on yourself. A big thing like that—losing someone you love in such gruelling circumstances—can leave its mark on a person. It's not all that easy to let go, is it?'

'Maybe it shouldn't be easy,' she finally said. 'Maybe forgiveness should be hard. Because then at least you know it's real.'

Tom nodded. 'It sounds therapeutic to me.'

But Maggie suddenly wasn't sure who she was talking

about forgiving any more. Her father or Carl. Or herself for letting *their* failings affect her so much.

'I have been watching this thing evolve for days now, and I still have no idea how you managed to turn all that swirling blue into something so fantastic,' he said, glancing her way. 'You really are one fine painter, Ms Bryce.'

His voice was soft, his face was full of wonder, and Maggie bit her lip to stop herself from blubbering all over him.

'One thing, though,' Tom said.

'Mmm?'

'Did you ever look that blue?' he asked, catching her completely off guard. So off guard in fact that she burst out laughing.

She laughed so long and so hard that she hiccuped at the end of it and even had to wipe away a couple of stray tears into the bargain. 'Don't be ridiculous.'

'Hey, I'm not the one who painted a blue face. Did you moonlight as an Arctic explorer? Or do you feel the cold more than most? Perhaps you've always harboured a secret wish to become a member of the Blue Man Group?'

'Tom, come on, this isn't funny,' she said.

'Who said it was?'

He was smiling at her. But it wasn't a cheeky smile. It was a doting smile. A compassionate smile. She watched in mute fascination as he lifted her hand and kissed the upturned palm. His hot lips, so gentle and so affectionate, burned a brand into her calloused skin. A brand she feared she would never be able to wash away.

Maggie didn't even realise she was crying until she tasted the salt of her tears in her mouth. And this time Tom didn't hesitate. Before she knew it, she was in his arms, those strong warm hands running up and down her back, over her hair, in a perfect wave of consolation and understanding.

'Maggie, sweetheart,' he said, 'it's okay. It'll be okay.'

He continued muttering the 'there, there' words she'd had to endure from so many friends over the years. Back when her dad had left, and again when her husband had cheated. But somehow, coming from this big strong man, she found herself hoping it might be true.

He kissed the top of her head before pulling away, and she fought against the urge to wrap her arms around his neck and hang on with all her might. She sniffed, the tears no longer coming, as if letting it all out in one fell swoop, the tension, the upset, the embarrassment had left her.

'All better?' he asked.

'Perfect,' she said. She took in a shaky breath and her focus narrowed to the moist patch her tears had left on Tom's grey T-shirt. Though her life was nowhere near perfect, it was looking up. She only wished she had more time, more money, that she'd been able to paint more than therapy on to the canvas, and that Portsea property wasn't quite so very pricey.

She risked looking up at Tom. 'Thank you,' she said, making sure to hold on to his gaze with all her strength.

'For what?' he asked, his voice gravelly as he used both hands to sweep her messy hair out of her eyes.

'Being here. Being the first man in my life who didn't run the moment everything looked like it was about to get too hard.'

His hazel eyes flickered left to right and back again, as though he was trying to tell her something he couldn't put into words. But didn't say a word.

Maggie's confidence slipped, just a bit, but enough to let in a whole new load of self-doubt. She gave herself a good mental shake. For, no matter how good he'd been to her tonight, how kind, how sweet, how present, he *had* run before. He hadn't left Sydney looking for a change of pace, he'd run from himself. And she had no guarantee he wouldn't do so again.

To save face, and her wavering heart, she disentangled herself from his warm embrace and backed away. 'Look at the time! It must be after nine. I'm so sorry to have kept you. Why don't you head off?'

He tucked his hands in the back pockets of his jeans. 'Are you sure?'

She smiled up at him. 'I'm sure. I'll see you tomorrow, Tom.'

He gave her a small wave and jogged down the back steps and to his car.

And I'll see you the next day and the next, she thought. But could she count on seeing him the day after that? Looking deep inside herself, Maggie knew she had no idea. But things in her life were progressing such that she was at last beginning to believe that she could count on herself.

She took one last look at The Big Blue. The portrait was ambiguous, blurred, and so very blue. Just as she had felt for so very long.

She took the painting down from its pride of place on her easel and set it aside. It was time to start with a fresh canvas.

CHAPTER EIGHT

BY LUNCH time Tuesday the taste of the coming summer hung hot, humid and heavy in the air. Tom's back ached, he felt as if his knuckles had been cracked twenty times over and he would have given away the sizeable contents of his bank account for an hour-long shower. But the shower could wait, for he was a man on a mission.

He wiped his hands on the sides of his jeans and pulled a T-shirt over his sweat-lathered torso as he headed up Maggie's back stairs.

Seeing her crying the night before had twisted him into knots the likes of which he had never known. His urge to help, to fix, had gone into overdrive—so much he'd arrived before she was up and hadn't stopped during the six straight hours since.

He hoped the pay-off for all his hard work that morning would be worth it. He really did. But, even as he'd pulled weeds and yanked out tough vines and wrenched muscles he hadn't even known he had, he'd known that it was the least he could do.

'Maggie?' he called out from the back door, not wanting to clump mud inside.

After a pause he heard a small, 'Yep?'

'Are you ready for lunch?'

'Coming. Give me a minute,' she said, meaning he wouldn't have to follow through on his back-up plan to throw her over his shoulder and carry her downstairs in a fireman's lift if she tried to beg off lunch again. He wasn't sure if he was relieved about that or disappointed. 'You've been quiet out there today. Tom?'

Feeling silly having a faceless conversation, he wiped his muddy boots on the back mat and then made his way inside.

He looked up, ready to give her lip about the fact that he was used to her finding any excuse to walk away from The Big Blue, when he saw that The Big Blue was gone.

In its place was a new canvas, already lathered in deep forest-green and apricot so bright it was almost blinding. He looked up to her to ask what was going on, but all words stopped before they even hit his throat.

A red bandanna was tucked into her waistband, leaving her mass of pale brown hair scrunched up into a messy bun, which over the course of the morning had fallen into a sexy tumble of disarray. She wore a cream collared T-shirt which gave her skin a golden glow.

And below? Below were the shortest pair of short shorts a girl could wear without a health warning. They were khaki, cuffed and reached just below the swell of her buttocks, leaving bare a pair of long, smooth, shapely legs which went all the way to the floor.

'Hi,' Maggie said, wiping her hands on an old rag, her voice a little breathless.

Tom struggled to lift his eyes. 'How are you doing?' he asked.

'I'm okay. I'm fine. Truly.'

'I would have come up earlier to check on you, but I really wanted to get to work in a big way today.'

She gave him a small smile which told him she didn't believe a word of it. 'Tom, it's okay. I didn't expect you to come in and pat me on the hand and lather me with sympathy. In fact I would have hated it. I really do feel much better today. Great, in fact. On top of the world.'

He nodded. And stared at her a little more. At the wisps of sleek, soft hair hanging beside her fine jaw. At the small line of muscle along the length of her upper arm. Had she always been this stunning? He'd always thought her beautiful in a detached kind of way, but seriously, had she always been *this* beautiful?

'Sorry. Are you in some kind of rush?' she asked, her full mouth hooking into a shy smile.

This Maggie, this cool, self-assured, at ease Maggie was so intimidating it caused Tom to fall back on his own self-defence mechanism—innocuous flirtation.

'Nothing's wrong,' he said, shooting her a grin. As the blood returned to his feet he ambled to her side. 'I was just hoping you hadn't shaved for my sake.'

'Excuse me?' she said, her easy smile faltering.

He let his gaze drop and take pleasure in another eyeful of her graceful limbs, which had somehow managed to avoid the wrath of her flicking brush while her feet had still captured flecks of blue paint. 'I was momentarily blinded by the fact that you seem to have legs,' he admitted.

Maggie ingenuously tipped her toes in towards one another and looked down. 'You'd had your doubts?'

'More like suspicions, really. And I'm quite enjoying them being brought to light.'

She curled her lip to show that she wasn't all that impressed by his candour. 'You may have noticed that it's a bloody hot day. If you're allowed to work out there with your shirt off, then I'm allowed to wear shorts.'

Tom held up his hands in surrender. 'Hey, I'm not complaining.' He let his hands drop. 'So you've been watching me work, have you?'

A pretty pink blush grew in her pale cheeks as she only just realised what her comeback had revealed, and he caught a refreshing glimpse of the ruffled Maggie he knew and…liked.

'I have to make sure you're not out there slacking off on my dollar.'

'Of course you do,' he said.

'Anything else?' she asked, glaring at him and lifting a hand to her cocked right hip. 'Or can we go eat?'

'We eat. Outside.'

'Why?' Maggie said, but she was already cleaning her paintbrush in a jar of water, scrunching her toes on the drop cloth and retying her hair into a less messy high bun to keep her hair off the back of her neck. 'Didn't we just agree it's too hot?'

'*Why* is because you paid for dinner Saturday night and it pained my manhood, so I decided to make it up to you with something a bit special today.' That part was rubbish, but she didn't need to know that.

She met him at the back door. He faltered for a second when her heady perfume sneaked under his defences and curled itself around him.

Before he had the chance to second guess himself, he snaffled the bandanna from the waistband of her shorts, the tips of his fingers accidentally making contact with a small sliver of skin on her waist.

Okay, so it wasn't entirely accidental. But it was subtle. Subtle enough that she would have no idea how much he'd longed to touch her right there. Nor how much touching her there only made him want to touch her everywhere else.

When he moved back he saw that her eyes were closed. Not

mid-blink, but closed. They flittered open—grey, wide and expressive. Okay, so she knew.

He gave her an eloquent smile before reaching up and covering her eyes in the square of red cloth.

'Hey!' she cried, reaching up to grab at the bandanna.

'Uh-uh,' he said, peeling her hands away and tucking them at her sides. Her hands clenched in his, before slowly letting go. Trusting him…

He baulked at the thought, his fingers losing grip on the fabric for a brief moment. But he couldn't back out now. It would only make him look like an idiot. So he tied the bandanna over her eyes, then took her by the shoulders and led her down the back steps, softly saying, 'Step. Step. Step,' until they reached level ground.

'Is this really necessary?' she asked as they made their way across the expanse of dirt.

For an answer he moved her slightly to the left to make sure she was in the prime position, then let her go. She wobbled slightly on her bare feet, then tilted her head in his direction.

'Am I to remove my blindfold yet, or are you in fact about to push me over the cliff in some sort of effort to put me out of my misery? Because I wasn't kidding earlier. I really am fine. It's a female thing. A good cry solves all ills.'

Tom laughed. 'I'd never condescend to think myself well-adjusted enough to judge anyone else's misery.'

He allowed himself a couple of long moments to watch her, unnoticed. The long legs, the straight back, the paint-splattered feet. Her messy hair, her delicate neck, the determined, understated strength that for some reason he had only now begun to notice.

'Go ahead,' he said, his voice overly hoarse. 'Take it off.'

She lifted her hands and peeled the red fabric over her head.

Her mouth dropped open and her eyes grew wide as she took in the picnic blanket, the open cooler filled with prawns and fresh cob bread and the bottle of wine and array of exotic cheeses.

And the view to the cliff's face and beyond through the long thin tunnel he had spent the morning clearing.

She turned slowly. 'You did all this just this morning?'

'Well, hardly,' Tom said, smiling as her grey eyes sparkled back at him. 'I bought the prawns last night and the wine I've had in my cellar for a couple of years and—'

Maggie's right hand sneaked out and thumped him on the shoulder with such speed he didn't have the chance to get out of the way. 'Ow!' he cried. For a slight woman she packed quite a punch.

'I didn't mean that,' she said, flapping a hand at the cooler. 'I mean that!' She waved her arm in front of her, beyond the visual feast, to the slender view of the deep blue ocean before her.

She stepped over the picnic blanket and walked down the cool green tunnel towards the cliff's edge, taking care to keep her arms folded to escape the scrapes and cuts of the brambles reaching out to her from the high thorny walls.

The view *was* stupendous. Craggy cliffs zigzagged off to their left, while the Mornington beaches curled away to their right. The blue-green ocean lay flat and deep and full of mystery before them, cut through with the odd jetty, pier or sand bar. And, though Tom knew he really couldn't take the responsibility for all that, he found himself sidling up next to her, so that he could watch her face as she took it all in.

And it hit him like a sandbag to the diaphragm—where Maggie Bryce acrimonious was intriguing, and Maggie Bryce dolled up and laughing for the cameras was a stunner, Maggie Bryce relaxed and happy was heart-stoppingly lovely.

'Worth it?' Tom asked.

She coughed out an overwhelmed laugh. 'Are you kidding?' Oh, yeah, it had been worth the backache, the sweat and the sore muscles when the pay-off was that wide happy smile.

Then suddenly, before he even felt her shift, Maggie turned and hugged him. Tight.

Surprised out of his reverie, Tom stiffened in her arms. But it was only a split second before he gave in and hugged her right on back. The relief at having her in his arms again was explosive, connecting her to him in ways deeper than just the contact of flesh and skin. Soothing him, creating warmth deep within his abdomen. By the time he realised the feeling he was experiencing was the slow-burning realisation that he never wanted to let her go, it was too late to stop it.

Maggie cleared her throat of whatever emotion had sent her flying into his arms and, with her head bowed, moved out of his arms and stepped away.

Not quite sure what to do next, Tom moved away himself and shoved his hands into the back pockets of his jeans and kicked at a tuft of grass.

'Come on, sunshine,' he said, his voice dropping to a throaty whisper despite his jocular words. 'Even if that view of yours is enough to sustain you, I've never worked so hard in my life as I have this morning. *I'm* starved.'

'Sure. Sorry, of course,' Maggie said, skipping back to the picnic blanket and seating herself down like a good girl. Tom passed her a cushion. She took it without looking him in the eye.

The air around them buzzed with the oncoming of summer bees. Every now and then the high screech of a seagull split the air. Tom topped up her wine whenever it seemed too low. He passed over paper napkins when her fingers dripped with too much prawn juice. And at one stage he shifted slightly to make sure her face was protected from the worst of the heat.

'Do you know what a belvedere is?' Maggie asked out of the blue, staring up at her big ramshackle house, shielding her eyes from the sun.

'It's another name for a gazebo sited to command a fine view,' Tom said automatically, quoting from whatever university text book in which he'd first seen the word.

'That's what I thought,' she said, not even seeming to wonder how a guy like him knew something like that. 'Somebody somewhere had a sense of humour. This rambling house of mine has to be a hundred times bigger than any gazebo I've ever seen.'

'Though they got the view part right.'

Maggie spun about and looked out at the deep blue sea over his shoulder and sighed. 'That they did.'

'Is this what you were hoping for when you called me?'

She lifted her shoulders and let them slump again. 'I'm not all that sure what I was hoping for. Clarity, perhaps. A sign to tell me what move to make next.'

'Next?'

She glanced at him, something flashing across her eyes too quickly for him to catch it before it was gone and she was eyes down, pouring another glass of wine.

'Whether to sell up and move back to the city. I can likely get work teaching back there if it comes to that. But I'd really rather not. This place has begun to get its hooks into me, the way the girls warned me it would.' She turned and shot him a half smile. 'And the way it has hooked you.'

But Tom hadn't heard all that much past the notion that she might sell up and move back to the city. Melbourne was not much more than an hour's drive away, but he just knew that if Maggie left, if she went back to that life, if she once more became the glossy ice-blonde in the head to toe black, he would never hear from her again.

'But you can't leave now,' he said, trying his best to keep it light. 'You've only just begun to imbibe the culinary magnificence that is the Mornington Peninsula. First Tom Campbell signature reheated fettuccini, then The Sorrento Sea Captain's beer-battered fish. There are at least a dozen other fine, and not so fine, eateries only a ten minute drive from here. I cannot allow you to even think about leaving until you've tried them all.'

Maggie looked down at the peeled prawn in her hand and said, 'You've been terribly good to me, Tom Campbell. Above and beyond any handyman I've ever known.'

She smiled up at him, her eyes clear, missing their usual guarded edge. Tom's hands, which were engaged in a struggle with a cheap napkin, stopped moving. He felt the need to take in an extra large breath to fill his lungs. For he wasn't all that sure where he fitted with this new Maggie. This confident Maggie.

'You wouldn't think so if you knew how hard it has been for me not to grab that prawn from your hand and eat it myself. They were really all for me, you know. I just thought if you looked out your window and saw me eating them I'd never be forgiven.'

'Is that so?' Maggie laughed and the infrequent sound floated away on the ocean breeze. She went back to her prawn and Tom wondered if she had any clue that he was being *nice* in an effort to stop himself from being the complete opposite. His fingers itched to tangle themselves in her soft messy hair so he could better see into her eyes. They itched to run gently over her full bottom lip. His lips itched to move in, to kiss away the tangy taste of seafood sauce filling her mouth.

And then the phone rang.

Their eyes shot to the upstairs room.

'Any idea who that might be?' Tom asked.

Maggie uncurled her lanky form from the picnic blanket and dusted off her short shorts. 'Not a clue. A wrong number in all likelihood, but I'd better go see just in case.'

A slow warm smile lit her face as her eyes roved over their secluded little haven. 'Thank you for today, Tom. I'm touched. Truly. It's the nicest thing anyone has done for me in as long as I can remember.'

'It was my pleasure.'

Maggie loped away, taking her long legs and her enveloping perfume with her, leaving Tom feeling a bit daft alone on his little picnic blanket.

Maybe it was a wrong number? Or the paint store telling her they'd restocked a colour she was waiting on. Or maybe she was so eager to run up and get the damned thing because it could be Carl in Melbourne, now that Tom himself had cleverly gone and told her it would do her good to forgive the bastards who'd screwed her over.

He threw the half-peeled prawn back into his cooler. He suddenly wasn't hungry any more.

Maggie jogged up the back stairs and answered the phone.

'Maggie Bryce speaking.'

'Ms Bryce, it's Constance from Home Sweet Home. Just to let you know the coffee-coloured lounge suite you were eyeing the other afternoon has come off hold. So, if you want it, it's yours.'

Maggie grinned into the phone and moved to lean against the edge of the window frame so she could watch Tom pack up the remains of their beautiful picnic.

'You bet I want it, Constance.'

CHAPTER NINE

WEDNESDAY lunch time, Tom switched off the chipper he'd rented from Alex to clean up the mess he'd cleared so far.

He'd thought he'd heard the heavy strains of a truck engine coming up Maggie's driveway. And he hadn't been wrong. A furniture removal truck was making hard work of her twisted, weed-riddled drive.

'Now what has she gone and done?' Tom dropped his goggles and gloves to the ground and walked up the side of the house to meet the driver and Smiley and a jubilant Maggie at the front door.

'What's going on?' Tom asked.

'Come here,' she said, grabbing him by the arm and yanking him around the back of the truck where Rod Johnson, co-owner of a local homeware store, was opening wide the back doors.

And inside? Furniture. Bubble-wrapped, cloth-covered, brand-new furniture. The relief Tom felt was palpable. The burning in his lungs dissipated to a dull smarting. She wasn't leaving him just yet. *Portsea.* She wasn't leaving Portsea.

'Hey, Ms Bryce. Hey, Tom,' Rod said as he and his friend slid a great brown couch off the back of the truck.

'Morning, Rod,' Tom said.

'Just put it anywhere in the great room,' Maggie said. 'We'll figure it all out later.'

'Mind the ferns on the way in,' Tom said. 'They're vicious.'

Maggie gave Tom another little shove towards the truck and said, 'Come on. Use those muscles for some real hard labour for once.'

Feeling strangely euphoric now he knew that furniture was coming into her house and not going out, Tom grabbed the hand shoving at him and twisted it behind her back, until they were face to face, chest to chest, toe to toe.

'I don't remember furniture moving being part of our contract, Ms Bryce,' he said.

'Contract schmontract,' she shot back, eyes shining as she grinned back at him. She didn't even try to pull away or twist her way out of his grip. If anything she sunk closer to him, her body melting against his of its own accord. 'This will be the help of a *friend*.'

'Mmm,' he said. 'A friend, am I? Lucky me.'

He let go of her arm and she slowly let it sink to her side. Then she spun him around and shoved him up into the truck. 'Go, go, go! We don't have all day.'

An hour later, the truck was gone, the furniture was unpacked and bubble-wrap lay in a pile in the corner of the room.

'It looks like a real lounge room now, doesn't it?' Maggie asked.

'It really does.'

'Do you like?' she asked, her eyes as bright as new silver dollars as they skimmed appreciatively over her new things.

'I like very much. But why now all of a sudden?' he asked.

She opened her mouth to answer, then snapped it shut. Then, with a small breath in and out, she seemed to come to some sort of decision to tell him. She gave a small shrug. 'A couple of my paintings were used in a National Gallery calendar this year and some royalties came through. So I kind of splurged.'

'You kind of did,' he agreed.

'All I wanted was a stereo, but I fell in love with the couches. And then I went a bit overboard.' Her brow furrowed ever so slightly. 'Though I'm sure they'd give me a refund on the cushions and vases if I took them back today—'

'Maggie. It's all fine. Let yourself enjoy it.'

'Right. You're right.' She nodded. But she began biting at her bottom lip and flicking at her fingernails.

Tom realised he'd never really come to any conclusion about why she didn't have any furniture in the first place. He'd liked the idea that it was an eccentric artist thing. It was just another facet to her singular personality. But now he wondered; could it possibly be that since she was in the middle of a divorce, she was struggling to make ends meet?

It made sense. The idea that she might have to sell up and move back to Melbourne to teach. Repayments on a place like this couldn't come cheap. And it explained the way she was scrunching her toes nervously against the floor and glaring at the coffee table as though it had offended her.

She *could* downsize. But then again it was doubtful that the next tenant would only want to clear the brambles. They'd have a wrecking ball and a bulldozer in here so fast... And he didn't want to see that happen to Belvedere any more than she did. He'd grown attached to the place.

But, before Tom had the chance to even begin to think of finding a way to broach the subject, a cacophony of female voices came scrambling through the front door.

Of course. It was Wednesday.

'I'll go heat up lunch,' Tom said, gathering up the bulk of the bubble wrap in his arms and kicking the rest into the kitchen before him, leaving Maggie to brace herself against the juggernaut.

She stopped fussing and worrying as she experienced a whole new ripple of excitement as she waited for her friends to enter her brave new world.

'Maggie, you are not going to believe…' Freya's words petered out. Sandra banged into Freya's back as her legs failed her.

'Freya, move!' Sandra said, before she saw what had made Freya stop. 'Wooooooooooow!'

'Oh, Maggie,' Freya cried, 'what have you done?'

'She's finally bought herself some furniture, the love,' Ashleigh said, her eyes glowing as they scanned the measure and shape of the new forms in the room. She eased past Freya, running her sculptor's hands over the sloping back of the couch and letting her feet slide along the new plush pile red rug. Sandra skipped about the room, picking up cushions and looking into vases to check if the bouquets of red gerberas were real. They weren't.

'Why don't you ladies take a seat?' Tom said, coming in from the kitchen with a bottle of wine and a bottle-opener. 'Lunch is on its way.'

He dumped them into Maggie hands, grinned his potent knee-weakening grin, then went back from whence he came.

'Come on, girls,' Maggie said, feeling feisty and in charge for a change, and liking it. 'Do as the man says.'

She sat at the head of her new rustic eight-seater dining table, tossing the cork in the air. Freya looked from the empty kitchen doorway and back to her as if she had suddenly grown an extra head. Little did any of them know that

Maggie felt as if she had too. And she was loving every second of it.

'Sit, Freya,' she insisted. 'Today I feed you.'

Freya moved into the room and sniffed the air. Her face relaxed a little as she realised how edible it smelled. 'Your friend Tom's done all the cooking?'

'If that's all right with you,' Maggie said, delighted that Freya had accidentally said something nice about him.

Freya frowned again. 'No, seriously, Maggie. You'll poison us. Unless you're making sandwiches, in the very least you'll make us ill.'

'Relax. It was all Tom. I promise not to even help stir. Now, shut up, sit down and prepare to feast.'

Maggie got up from her seat and padded towards the kitchen. Tom was cooking up a tomato pasta storm. The scents bombarding her made her mouth water.

'It smells fabulous,' she said, reaching into the bubbling tomato sauce for a fingerful. Tom slapped her hand away before she got more than a drop.

He'd already made a mess of her kitchen; half the utensils were dirty and there were red splattered bowls aplenty, but she'd never seen her kitchen look so fabulous. Who was she kidding? She'd never seen the world look so fabulous as she had that day.

'Are they sitting?' Tom asked.

'Nope. I think they're in shock.'

'I hope they'll still eat.'

'Oh, they'll eat. I've never known three women so fond of eating. But first they'll have to go over every piece of furniture with an artist's eye and then give me their honest opinions.'

'Not the shy, retiring types, are they?' Tom asked.

'Not hardly. But I hope you'll stay for lunch this time. And that you'll like them, even after spending more than five minutes in their company.' Maggie licked the spot of tomato sauce off her finger before it dripped on to the floor.

'Is it so important that I like them?' he asked, stirring away.

Maggie stopped with her finger to her mouth. The weightlessness in her heart dissipated as she thought back over what she had said.

She'd woken in such a good mood, such a light-hearted mood, such a playful, hopeful mood, she'd forgotten that the rest of the world hadn't changed overnight as she had.

Sure she was still married, but even if she wasn't, Tom was still wholly unavailable. Whereas she knew right down deep in her heart that finally she was done running, she felt just as strongly that Tom wasn't. It seemed it would take constant reminding to remember it.

'I…I just want to make sure all of my friends get along,' she said.

'Right,' he drawled. 'I forgot we were now friends.'

'Well, yes. Of course we are. I don't let just anybody use my precious saucepan.'

'*You* don't even use your precious saucepan.'

'Well, I'm just saying—'

'That it's important to you that your friends like me.' He winked at her. 'Okay. I get it.'

Before Maggie could qualify that comment, Tom placed a pile of dinner plates into her arms, spun her on the spot and gave her a shove towards the dining room.

She had a dining room! A lounge suite. A rug. And somehow even her painting corner didn't look so much like an island, but like a piece of living art in itself.

'I can't believe you spent all this money in one hit,' said Freya. 'Unless…did you sell something new? Oh, Maggie that would be wonderful news.'

'Ah, no,' Maggie said, her voice quiet and soft, doing her best not to let it carry to the kitchen. 'Just some royalties.'

'Well, that's great too. So does that mean you're out of the red? Are you here to stay?'

'Well. No. Not yet.'

'Maggie…' Freya began.

'I bought this stuff because I wanted it, Freya. I thought it about time to surround myself with things that make me happy. Even if I only get to enjoy them for a couple of weeks, at least I'll have those couple of weeks. You're the one who was so insistent I reconnect with myself. Well, *myself* wanted a couch.'

'Leave her be, Freya,' said Sandra. 'It's her money. Her life. She can glue every last cent to one of her paintings and call it art if she wants.'

'Thank you, Sandra,' Maggie said.

'Right. But you should have bought red couches. These just blend way too much in here,' Sandra said.

Maggie felt steam rising. She loved these guys. Really she did. But they really could be an overbearing bunch of so-and-sos. 'So what do you think of my new stuff?' she asked Ashleigh.

Ashleigh smiled, patted her on the cheek and said, 'I think it's about time.'

Maggie nodded. 'Me, too. I'm done with marking time and saving my pennies and waiting for the other shoe to drop, guys. You all promised coming here would help me turn over a new leaf. And this is how I've turned. Like it or lump it.'

The room grew silent bar the thumping of a pulse in Maggie's head. The sound of a spoon scraping against a saucepan in the kitchen beyond broke the deathly quiet. Tom was right, she thought, picturing him whistling softly and pretending not to listen—they weren't the shy, retiring types. But then, stuff it, neither was she.

'Well, you definitely need a vase in that far corner. I've got just the one. In cream. Reflective glaze,' said Freya, which for Freya was as much as giving in.

And Maggie could have hugged her.

An hour later the four of them sat back on Maggie's couches. Replete. Maggie had her feet up on the coffee table, Sandra's feet were dangling over the armrest and Freya was cross-legged and comfortable. And Maggie wished for about the eighteenth time that day that she had just gone ahead and done this months ago.

'This has been fun, guys, but it's time for me to get to work,' Tom said, peeling his long body from a dining chair he'd dragged over beside the couch.

Maggie watched with a small smile on her face as he lifted the chair and placed it back where it belonged. And she knew the reason she hadn't bought herself a house full of furniture six months before was because she had been at a loose end. Until Tom had come along and simply advised her not to expect the worst any more.

'My boss is a slave-driver,' Tom said, winking at her. 'If she knew I'd taken this long for lunch, I'd likely lose a limb.'

'Thanks, Tom,' the girls all called out at once, before lolling back into the soft chairs with mingled laughter.

He gave them a salute and a smile, saving his last look for Maggie. His smile changed, shifted, softened, warmed, lingered and then he was gone.

Maggie leant her elbows on her knees and her chin on her palms and enjoyed the calm before the storm. She'd known that inviting Tom for lunch would only cause dissent in the ranks, but that was just too bad. He'd been nothing but sweet to her and he deserved to be known for more than dating 'the American broad'.

But now they were alone, just her Wednesday girls and her, all bets were off.

'I hear rumours you had a date Saturday night,' Freya said before Tom was barely out the door.

'We had *dinner*,' Maggie said. 'Accidentally.' Even she heard the defensiveness in her voice and she wasn't surprised when the mood in the room shifted as shackles rose and sensitivities grew.

'Oh, what have you gone and done, Mags?' Freya asked, eyes wide and alarmed.

Here we go… 'I've done nothing.'

'Rubbish. You've done something. You slept with him.'

She shook her head. 'I did no such thing.'

'Then you've definitely kissed him,' Freya accused.

Maggie shook her head again. 'Nope. Haven't.'

'I know! I know! She's fallen in love with him,' Sandra said, slapping her hand over her mouth as though wishing to take the words back.

Maggie tried to shake her head. She really did. She squeezed and clamped her teeth tight and did her all to simply move her head left and then right, but found that her honesty meter was in high gear and she could not.

Freya's eyes squeezed shut tight. 'Oh, Maggie.'

'You've actually fallen for the hunk?' Sandra bubbled. 'With the muscles and the voice and those gorgeous eyes and the to-die-for pasta recipe and—?'

'The guy currently working at the bottom of my back stairs,' Maggie hissed. It was far too late before she realised what she had just admitted.

Sandra leapt out of the chair and clapped her hands and hugged Maggie until she could barely breathe.

'But you've known him—what? A week? Two weeks?' Freya asked.

'How long did it take for you to fall for the twins' father?' Maggie said. Freya's pale cheeks grew red and blotchy and Maggie knew it had been a low blow. But she was panicking. Because she *hadn't* fallen for Tom. She liked having him around, that was all. She liked that he always looked out for her. She liked the way he looked and the way he looked at her. She liked that he made her feel smart, funny, beautiful and talented, and she liked that he liked the fact that she was all those things.

What she *didn't* like was Freya looking at her as if she'd gone out of her mind. 'So I like him! A lot. More than a lot. Okay, so I'm crazy about him. That doesn't make me crazy. Does it?' *So much for waking up a new person. Oh, what had she gone and done?*

'Sandra, what do you think?'

Sandra unbuttoned her lips. 'I think he's hot.'

'Right. Excellent. Ashleigh?'

Ashleigh sat calmly upright in her chair. 'What we think isn't the topic here, my sweet. We are here to help you forage your way through your hormones and reservations to see what you think.'

'Tremendous. Helpful. Thanks.'

'No. This is all wrong. What about Carl?' Freya cried out, clutching at straws.

'What about him?' Maggie asked, her voice surprisingly calm considering Freya had deigned to use the 'C' word.

'Well, this guy's nothing like Carl,' Freya said, her voice shaky. 'He's…sweaty.'

And Maggie burst out laughing. Of all the things Freya could have come up with, that was it? 'Carl could be sweaty, Freya,' she said. 'He just didn't carry it off quite as spectacularly well as Tom does.'

Freya shuddered. 'I know Carl did an unforgivable thing to you, Maggie. But he's urbane and sophisticated. He understands the circles we run in. And, though you can be a real pain in the ass at times, his maturity meant that he never told you so once.'

'And how did that work out for her?' Ashleigh asked, as always appearing just at the opportune moment to shine the light of inspiration where it most needed to be shone.

Freya's mouth snapped shut. For after that there was nothing to say. Maggie let her feet drop to the floor, then moved sideways and reached out to hug her stiff friend.

'The truth was, that renowned maturity of his always frustrated the hell out of me,' Maggie said. 'I get moody. I get PMT. Heck, every now and then I am just plain grumpy. And he never said a word. I never really thought it was all that healthy for him to keep it all bunched up inside.'

'So how is it with Tom?' Sandra asked, asking the question that they'd been skirting around.

'Do you really want to know?' Maggie asked, her view glancing off Freya.

'Always,' Sandra insisted, leaning forward, her eyes bright with anticipation.

'With Tom I feel constantly on edge. My skin prickles and my hair itches whenever he's within view. When I bite, he bites right on back. When I tear up, he gets torn up himself. And when he comes within ten feet of me I want to eat up those ten feet and just throw myself into his arms and never let him go.'

Freya scoffed. Sandra sighed. And Ashleigh looked so deep into her eyes Maggie thought she might choke on the tenderness growing inside her. That was all she had intended to say, but once she'd started she found she couldn't stop.

'He's charming as all get out, but it's only to cover up the fact that deep down he's as scratched and dented as the rest of us. But he's instinctive and unaffected. And those eyes and those shoulders… You have to admit he's gorgeous.'

Ashleigh smiled. Sandra nodded. Even Freya raised an eyebrow in assent.

'Look, the simple fact of the matter is that every time I start a relationship I expect they'll hurt me and leave me and that's what happens. But, with Tom, I don't know, I haven't ever expected anything and he just keeps coming through.'

Maggie took a breath to tell them about the way he had held her in his arms two nights before, allowing her to let out a lifetime's worth of demons through her tears, and the picnic on the bluff he had created just for her, and the million small kindnesses he had given her every day since they'd met, but she swallowed the stories down.

They were precious memories. Beautiful memories. And there was no way she was going to offer them up for Freya's ridicule. Or to make poor Freya feel even sadder about the love she'd never really managed for herself.

So, to put the subject matter at rest, Maggie took a deep breath and said, 'He figured out what The Big Blue is all about.'

'No, he can't have,' Sandra whispered, her eyes slamming sideways to the painting leaning at the base of her art table. 'So what is it?'

She felt Ashleigh's hand squeeze her thigh and she knew that Ashleigh, her best friend and mentor, had already known for some time.

'It's a self-portrait,' Maggie said before her throat closed over completely. 'It's me.'

Freya stood up in shock and Sandra leapt to her feet to have a closer look.

'Holy heck, he's right,' Freya finally said, her voice raw with emotion. 'How could we not have all seen it?'

Maggie shrugged. 'I don't know. But he saw it. Days ago. I told you, he's insightful. Scarily so.'

Freya's face closed down again. She slid on her knees in front of Maggie, taking both her hands. 'It's the sensitive ones that will let you down the hardest, Maggie. Believe me.'

'Nah, the sensitive ones only cry when you've had enough of them,' Sandra said, shaking her head in wonder as she sat with her nose an inch from The Big Blue. 'He's hot, Mags, but when you come to your senses it'll be a mess letting him go.'

'You're one in a long line of many, Maggie,' Freya said. 'I've been asking around about him. It's not just that horrible American woman last summer. He's a serial dater. A heartbreaker who targets unavailable women. He has more money than Midas and because of that thinks he can use people up and spit them back out again when he's done.'

'Freya, just stop. You're only doing yourself a disservice in brandishing all that rubbish. You don't know him,' Maggie said, her voice trembling. She pulled her hands away.

Freya flinched as though she'd been slapped. 'I need some air,' she muttered, before tearing from the couch and outside on to the balcony.

'She's a redhead, Mags, what do you expect?' Sandra lit up a cigarette and headed outside too.

'I was in love once,' Ashleigh said, once they were alone, and Maggie was certain she had heard wrong.

'You were in love?' With a man? Maggie wanted to ask, but she had the distinct feeling Ashleigh wasn't finished talking.

'I was thirty. His name was Robert. He was tall, with intelligent blue eyes that saw right through me. I was down for the count in an hour, and in his bed by the end of the night. It took me six months of bliss before the fog cleared enough for me to realise he was married.'

'Oh, Ash.' She could see in Ashleigh's eyes that she still loved this man. Twenty-odd years later and she had never moved on.

It seemed love was never an easy road. Was that what Ashleigh was trying to tell her—that it was just a vicious circle? Was that why she felt so much for Tom? Despite the huge differences between him and the type of men she had been with before, was there something about him that gave her that same deep down feeling? Was the very fact that he was emotionally unavailable the true reason why she was so drawn to him?

'I'd never take that six months back for all the tea in China,' Ashleigh said, running a finger down Maggie's cheek. 'Okay?'

Maggie nodded, but she wasn't all that certain what she was nodding about.

Freya came back inside all of a sudden, followed by Sandra, practically sprinting behind her.

And after them came Tom. He looked over the scattered group—Freya's pinched face, Sandra's open amusement and Ashleigh's cool appraisal. And, beneath the tan and stubble, Maggie was sure she saw him blush. 'Sorry to interrupt your natter, guys. I was just getting myself a cup of coffee. Anyone else thirsty?'

Smiley whimpered at the front door. Maggie looked up. Smiley never whimpered. He was the worst guard dog in history. The others didn't hear it. Ashleigh was busy putting in an order for tea, Freya mumbled something about needing a strong black coffee and Sandra was batting her eyelashes and following Tom into the kitchen to help.

Maggie got to her feet and moved to the open front door. A warm wind slithered against her face. And Smiley, standing, looking outward, whimpered and wagged his tail.

'Smiley, what's the—?' Maggie didn't need to ask any more as the reason behind Smiley's excitement was standing in her doorway.

'Carl?'

CHAPTER TEN

TOM followed Sandra back out of the kitchen, blowing cool air across a mug of coffee he'd made for Maggie.

But she wasn't sitting curled up on the couch as she had been when he'd walked into the great room minutes before. She was standing in the open doorway talking to a man with salt-and-pepper hair, an expensive-looking suit and a purple tie.

Maggie looked once over her shoulder at the group before grabbing the guy by the jacket sleeve and dragging him outside. Smiley even dragged himself up and followed them. And then the front door slammed shut.

Tom made a move to call attention to the goings on to the other girls when he suddenly realised where he had seen the man before. Salt-and-pepper hair. Expensive suit. In the photographs at the art gallery on the Internet.

That was her husband. The shmuck who had robbed those molten silver eyes of their permanent shine.

Tom snapped his mouth shut and let his hand slump until Maggie's hot coffee came to rest on the dining table with such a bump that coffee sloshed out over the sides.

He looked at the girls—Freya was frowning and sweeping up a mess of crumbs from the rustic table top, while Sandra was sitting at the dining table poking her in the side with her finger. But Ashleigh was watching him with a slight smile on her face. He knew there was no point feigning innocence around this woman. She was some kind of witch or something.

'Was that Carl?' he asked.

Ashleigh nodded.

'Was what Carl?' Freya of the big ears asked.

Tom tensed and glanced to the front door. Freya saw it. 'He's here?' she hissed.

Sandra pushed her chair back with a loud scrape. 'The sleazoid rat bastard. Leaving our Maggie all broken-hearted and destitute, while he schleps about town with all his money and her bastard friends. Let me at him.'

Ashleigh held out a hand and Sandra shut up.

But Tom saw it all only peripherally; his vision was blurred as he dug his fingernails into his palms and tried to listen through twenty feet of open space and a closed front door to what could possibly be being said between salt-and-pepper Carl and the bright and beautiful woman he had treated so badly.

Maggie moved Carl away from the door and away from any possibly straining eyes and ears, though her heart thumped so hard against her ribs she could barely hear her own words above it.

'How's Becca?' was the first thing that came into her head, though she wondered how she'd react if he smiled and said she was still a size six with an adorable bump and not a varicose vein in sight.

'She's in the hospital, Mags. She came prematurely,' he said, before he even said hello. 'Eight weeks early. The baby is still in the ICU.'

The *baby*. After all the pain and suffering and recriminations and blame, and trying so hard to be a family, or fix a family, out there somewhere there was now a baby—fighting for its life. Maggie automatically held out a hand to Carl and then remembered who he was and what he had done to her. Her hand shrunk back to her side.

'Is she okay?' No matter what he'd done, she would never have wished that on him, or Becca, or especially Becca's tiny baby.

'She spends most of her time at the hospital,' he said. She thought she saw a minuscule shrug, and that truly reminded her who she was talking to. Urbane, sophisticated, imperturbable Carl. So very cool and untouchable, like her father had been before him. She wondered how she had never seen any of that before. But then she'd never really known anybody to compare that kind of man with. Until now.

'He's so very, very tiny.'

He. She clutched her T-shirt to her stomach. They'd had a little boy.

'Small, like Becca,' he continued, clueless as always as to the emotions stirring inside her. 'Funny, I always imagined my first boy to be strapping and strong. Like you.'

'Me? Strong? It hardly takes a strong person to run away from home.'

'You never ran, Maggie. I forced you out. It was cruel. And childish. But I wanted you to feel how I'd been feeling for years.'

'What's that supposed to mean?'

'For the last years of our marriage I felt like a fifth wheel. You knew what you wanted and went for it. And when you succeeded you didn't need me any more. My connections. My money.'

'Carl, that's a terrible thing to say.'

'It's the truth. But it's not your fault, it's mine. I was

looking for someone soft to nurture, and you thought you were looking for a man to look after you. But you never really needed anything of the sort.'

'So is that why you screwed around on me? Because I wasn't *soft* enough for you?'

He winced at her choice of words, and she was glad. Because she couldn't believe this man who'd shared her life for ten years had no idea how soft she really was. She was so soft that in the early days of their separation she'd felt as if the only thing keeping her upright was her clothes. She was so soft that all she'd ever really wanted from him was his love. And she wondered now if she'd ever even really had that.

And, in that moment, Maggie felt finally, fully and dizzily released. She had outgrown the need for a father figure, but he'd never outgrown the need to be the carer, sole breadwinner, the head of the house, and likely never would. It wasn't such a bad trait for a guy to have, it just wasn't the trait that she needed or wanted in her man.

About to ask him again why he'd come, she saw that he was leaning back, looking blankly through the foliage to the front picture windows. His brow was furrowed and his eyes hooded and looking somewhere off to her left.

She glanced over her shoulder to find the gang mid-argument as usual. Sandra was waving a linen napkin at Freya, who was ducking out of the way, Ashleigh was clapping her hands to silence them and Tom was seated on the edge of the dining table, sipping from a cup of coffee, his gaze faraway. A smile tugged at the corner of her mouth before she realised Carl was watching her.

'Who's the guy?' His eyes focused on her face for the first time since he'd shown up at her doorstep.

'He's a friend,' she said on a faint sigh.

She saw a flare of pain flash across their clear blue depths and then it was gone. He'd just seen a glimpse into her new life. The life she'd made for herself down here. He'd seen she wasn't pining away without him, and without his money. She was moving on with her life. And it was time he did too.

'Carl, do the right thing by all of us and sign the divorce papers, send them to my lawyer and go home to your girlfriend and child.'

She reached out and squeezed him on the shoulder. And then her natural caring instincts came to the fore and she gave in and hugged him. Carl hugged her back, comforting in his familiarity, but even more comforting in that she felt not one spark in his arms. Not one itch. Not one desire to ever be in that position again.

She'd done the right thing in leaving when she had, in asking for not one cent of Carl's money in the settlement, just the clothes on her back, the car in her driveway, the dog on her front doorstep and the equity in the house sending its long protective shadow over her now.

She pulled away and took a step back. 'Goodbye, Carl. Tell Becca my prayers are with you all.'

And then she turned her back on her old life for the last time.

The minute Maggie came back inside, Ashleigh stood and said, 'Right, well we'd better be off.'

Freya and Sandra stopped bickering and looked as surprised that their visit had been cut short as Maggie was. But they did as they were told. They stood, grabbed their gear in record time and headed to say their goodbyes.

Tom stood too. Though he wasn't all that sure he wanted to get within hitting distance of Freya, who had been shooting daggers with her eyes all afternoon, so he hovered in the background.

But one by one they came to him.

'Thanks for lunch. It was ace. Be good,' Sandra whispered, as she stood on tiptoe to kiss him on the cheek.

'I heard you were the one who put the new roof on the Jamesons' pergola after the storm tore it right off. Nice job,' Freya said, barely looking him in the eye.

Ashleigh sauntered over to him last of all. 'I like you, Tom Campbell,' she said, and again it felt as if her pale eyes could see all the way into the back of his mind.

'I like you too, Ashleigh Caruthers,' he said.

'Mmm. Just make sure you don't go doing anything to change my good opinion, you here.'

Tom offered a closed mouth smile as she walked away. Somehow all three of them had been trying to tell him something, but it was a darned pity it was in some sort of secret code that would take him days and a sex change operation to figure out.

Then, as if in a puff of smoke, the coven was gone. And Maggie was wandering back in, her steps a little woozy as though she was punch drunk.

With a faraway sort of smile on her face, she pulled her hair from its messy bun, but this time she scratched her skull for several seconds before simply letting it cascade down her back in a dishevelled disarray.

Tom turned to watch her as she moved past him to the dining table and picked up a couple of dirty teacups. If he didn't know that it was physically impossible, he could have sworn she was floating about two inches off the ground as she took them into the kitchen.

Tom, on the other hand, felt as if he had lead in his shoes.

'So that was Carl,' he said, following her and leaning in the kitchen doorway, the tension in his voice unmistakable.

She turned and some of the glow about her faded. But not all. 'Mmm hmm,' she said. 'That was Carl.'

'He's a dashing sort of bloke,' Tom said.

'I've always thought so,' she said, her eyes narrowing a tiny little bit.

'So what did he have to say for himself?'

Maggie crossed her arms and stared at him, but her voice was still even. 'What's with the twenty questions?'

'A guy's not allowed to make conversation?'

'Conversation? Sure. Interrogation? Not so much. Whatever it is you are trying to say, spit it out.'

If she wasn't going to be angry at the guy for cheating on her and leaving her destitute, as Sandra had let slip, then he sure as heck would be angry for her. He looked down at the dirt beneath his fingernails, hoping to find more clarity there.

'I'm trying to figure out how you can swan in here all sweetness and light when the guy who broke your heart and took your home and crushed your hopes and your dreams just showed up on your doorstep after six months of no contact.'

'Would you prefer me to be in tears?'

'I'd prefer you to be pissed off!'

Her cheeks grew pink, her eyes blazed. And he knew that she was finally pissed off. At *him*.

'And what if I'd choose not to be pissed off? What are you going to do about it?' she asked.

She raised one fine eyebrow. That small move was so damned sexy it was all Tom could do to keep his mind on track. But he was picking a fight and now he was on a roll he intended to keep on picking.

He moved fully into the kitchen, needing to be nearer her,

even if those fists were looking ready to strike. He did his best to ignore her perfume, though with every inward breath he felt it winding itself more tightly around him.

'Maggie, he should know about the nice life you have made for yourself out here, and it should eat away at his insides every time he thinks about it. He should know about The Big Blue and how it took for you to leave him to find it in yourself to paint such a thing. He should know how you were the one with the guts to start a new life without having to hurt the people closest to you along the way. I, for one, have never seen anything braver.'

There, that ought to do it. If she couldn't figure out from that little speech that it was his job to stick up for her at all costs after that, then she'd never get it.

Maggie swallowed, her lean pale throat working hard, her grey eyes flicking back and forth between his as she let his words sink in.

'You think I was too quick to forgive him, don't you?' she asked. 'You think Carl should be made to pay for what he did? You think he should burn for it for all his remaining days?'

'You bet I do.'

'Because that's how you think you ought to be punished for not being with Tess when she died?'

'Sorry, what?' Tom said, mentally backtracking.

'Tom,' Maggie said, taking him by the hand and drawing him inches closer. 'My coming from Melbourne is one thing—I mean, the house was mine and Melbourne's an hour away by car, but you moved states, you moved from the fastest city in Australia to a place with all the excitement factor of a sloth on Valium. Do you think Tess would be all that happy about the fact that you are hiding down here?'

'This conversation isn't about me,' he said. He was meant to be grilling her. Not the other way around.

'Come on, Tom. Think about it. Think about what you do here. Think about what you've done for me. You couldn't fix her. So *that's* why you quit working in restorations to become a handyman. So that you could fix things for everyone else instead.'

He wondered for a moment if she'd been talking to Alex. 'I did, I do, but that's not why. I like working with my hands and—'

'Crap,' she said, letting go of his hand so quickly he almost stumbled.

'Excuse me?' Tom said, on a short bark of laughter.

She turned to the sink and began to rinse the coffee cups and tomato splattered dinner plates. 'That's just a big pile of crap.'

Tom leaned his hip against the bench to give himself purchase, and had a sudden wash of *déjà vu*. That first morning in this very kitchen, as he'd decided whether doing a job for this woman would be worth the effort. He now knew that the effort he'd envisaged was only a millionth of the effort he'd put in so far. And he was *still* wondering if it really had all been worth it.

'You can't fix me and then move on, you know, like some guardian angel.'

'Like some what—?'

But she cut him off again. She was on a roll.

'I don't need a father figure, Tom. And I don't need a guardian angel. I need friends, and I need relationships that run on an equal footing. I'm not prepared to give more than I receive any more or vice versa, for that matter.'

Tom was rendered speechless. The last thing he'd wanted to do was find himself in a position where he again wanted to do all he could to make another person's life better. But that was where he was. Didn't she know that was some big deal for him? Wanting to help, to soothe, to placate, to make better? And that it had taken a pretty big emotional leap for him to go there at all?

Obviously not. Or, if she did know, she was making it plain that it was the last thing she wanted of him.

Tom stood upright on somewhat numb feet. His blood didn't quite know where to rush in that moment, for his heart was pumping it way too fast.

'Right,' he said. 'Okay. Now that we have that sorted, I'd better get back to work.'

'Mmm,' Maggie said. 'I hear your boss is a slave-driver. Better hop to it.'

'Right. Shall do.' And Tom walked away, more confused and angry and frustrated than he'd ever been in his entire life.

That night, Tom sat at the bar of The Sorrento Sea Captain. He was already halfway through his third beer when Alex came bustling in, his hair a mess and a baby food stain on the front of his shirt.

'Okay, call off the cavalry. I'm here.' Alex pulled himself up on to a barstool and motioned to the barman for the same as Tom. 'What's the big emergency?'

'I need some advice.'

Alex blinked. 'From me?'

'You're the only guy I know in a relationship that has survived longer than a footy season. So I'm sorry, mate, but you're it.'

'Right. Okay. Shoot.'

'It's about Maggie.'

'Tom…'

Tom held up a hand. 'Just hear me out, okay. No judgement. Not yet.'

Alex rearranged his ample buttocks more comfortably on the small round seat. 'I'm listening.'

'This afternoon she accused me of changing the Barclay sisters' smoke detector batteries as punishment for not being with Tess when she died.'

'And?'

'*And?*' Tom repeated, incredulous, turning on his chair to face his cousin down. 'You mean you agree?'

'Well, yeah. It doesn't take some sort of brainiac to figure that out. You and Tess were so tight. Best mates really. And no one took it harder when she died than you did. And then there's the architect thing. You were one. A big one. One who has made a lot of money and garnered a lot of respect doing it. And now you're driving a beaten up Ute, doing hard labour for a cheap buck that you don't even need. It's not such a stretch, Cuz.'

Tom sniffed in deep through his nose, then downed half a beer in one hit while he stared through the TV over the bar until his vision blurred.

'So is it *what* she said that has you all het up on this fine evening,' Alex asked, 'or the fact that Miss Hoity-Toity's the one who said it?'

'She's not hoity-toity,' Tom muttered.

'So what is she, then?'

What was she? Two weeks ago she had been no more to him than a spectre driving too fast down the main street in her big Jeep. Now she was…important. When had this suddenly become…that?

'She's no damsel in distress, that's for sure.'

Alex laughed. 'Well, what do you know?'

Tom put down his bottle and ran his hands over his mouth, back and forth, as though it could help him think. 'Believe it or not, fixing light bulbs has been enough for me these last years. That, fishing, sunshine, pasta and the occasional beer. You know as well as anybody that we have a good life here.'

'We do. But?'

'But since I met Maggie it's like I can see all the things missing from that perfect picture, like I've just discovered a hole left by a pulled tooth. And my tongue can't keep from playing with it.'

'Aside from the fact that she is a married woman—'

Tom glared at Alex, but he just glared right on back.

'Taking that out of the picture, what do you want from her? Are you suggesting this is a woman to be played with? Or is she more than that?'

Tom's eye twitched. 'We kind of had a row today. I was daft, and she was harsh. And it wasn't pretty. So isn't it too late to worry about all that?'

'You tell me.'

Tom let out a long slow breath and thought hard about what he wanted.

He didn't want a fling. What he felt for Maggie was beyond that. So far beyond he didn't know what to do with it. Because, for the first time in years, he felt parts of himself opening up. Emotional places he had thought long ago shut down and out of business for good. And with that he felt exposed. And exposure had a propensity to hurt. As such, everything inside screamed at him to just walk away.

'You really want my advice, Cuz?' Alex asked.

'Yeah,' Tom drawled. 'I really do.'

Alex laid a hand on his slumped shoulder. 'There's no point in even going there until you've forgiven yourself for Tess. You miss her, still. Heck, I miss her. And that's all right. That means that she'll never be forgotten. Her bad taste in music. Those awful pictures of horses she drew and gave us all for Christmas. The fact that she would have eaten corn-flakes for every meal if you'd let her. Keep that stuff close to your heart. But don't let the other stuff eat at your heart, or there'll be nothing left when the day comes that you need it.'

Tom looked at his cousin with new eyes. 'I never pegged you for a romantic, my friend.'

Alex downed the dregs of his beer in one gulp, threw a ten dollar note on the bar and disengaged himself from his seat. 'But, then again, what do I know? I'm just a small business owner from a small beach town who has six females in charge of the remote control. Any advice I give comes by way of Oprah and reruns of the *Gilmore Girls*.'

Tom laughed as he was meant to do, but as he watched Alex head out the door, in an obvious hurry to get back to those six females, he felt a hot shaft of something akin to envy pierce his chest.

Tom spent the next day working like a man possessed, not even stopping for lunch.

Maggie sneaked a peep out the window every now and then to check on his progress, and to check on him. She thought he was running his hands through his hair quite a bit more than usual, and that he was sweating as though it was five degrees hotter than it was, and she knew that after their argument the night before she was at least half to blame for his funk.

The brush was almost all gone. The view was as clear as it was ever going to get, and it was magnificent. The job was so close to done she could all but feel the sand beneath her feet. And it brought about equal amounts of excitement and gloom. For when the job was done, Tom would be her handyman no more.

She tried to think up ways to keep him a little longer. The cupboards in the spare bedrooms were a disgrace. And there was always that crazy wallpaper in the master bedroom. But she couldn't pay him, and she could hardly offer to keep him on with the promise of more paintings for the walls of his caravan, or wherever he lived.

In the meantime, Maggie spent the day packing up the Blue Smudge Series in the bubble-wrap that had come with her new furniture. Then she called a courier to collect them for her delirious agent. If Nina could flog them off for a hundred bucks apiece, that would give her another week's mortgage payment. Woohoo!

One piece she was loathe to pack was the piece she had started less than four days before. It was finished and it was beautiful. And where The Big Blue was a contemplation of her face, this new painting was very definitely a reflection of her heart.

The greys and shadowy greens and slashing apricot sky were a snapshot, a moment in time. She'd mixed a little vinegar and wood stain into the paint to give it the same sensory texture she'd experienced when living the moment the first time around. A slice of white split the canvas—the railing of the Sorrento Pier—and resting large and strong and familiar over the edge were Tom's beautiful hands.

It wasn't quite a landscape and wasn't quite a portrait, but it was a true blue Maggie Bryce original. She packed it up all the same, as it had the biggest chance of making her any money. And that had become more important to her than anything—to stay rather than hang on to the past.

The man in question came up to say his goodbyes just on sunset. 'I'm done.'

The way he said it, the finality in his words, had Maggie's breath hitching in her throat. 'Done for the night? Or *done* done?'

'*Done* done. Finished. Contract fulfilled.' He was stiff. His eyes dark. His lazy smile nowhere in evidence. She could tell he was still upset about their discussion the day before. About Carl. And Tess. And about a lot of things she'd love to help him sort through, if only he gave her the chance.

'You still have another day, if you need it,' she said, trying to act cool, but the speed with which the words came negated her performance.

Tom's cheek twitched. 'There's a little cleaning up to do, but for all intents and purposes the pathway is cleared. Though I didn't do a dry run down to the beach, as I thought you might want that honour yourself. Do you want me to take you down there now?'

That would mean this whole thing coming to an end. Then and there. And Maggie was not even nearly ready for that. She'd thought she'd get at least another day. She needed at least another day. Hell, if she was honest with herself, she'd need at least another millennium before she was ready to see this guy leave for good.

'Not tonight. I think I'd rather leave it for morning, when we can enjoy it better. Smiley and me,' she added.

'Right. I'll see you, then.' He made a move to leave.

'Do you want to take The Big Blue now, or tomorrow?' she asked, motioning to the one painting she hadn't sent away.

His eyes darted over the empty corner. 'Where are the others?'

'Gone,' she said with a shrug. 'Off to market.'

'You've sold them?' he asked, a glimmer appearing in his dark hazel eyes for the first time in hours.

'Not yet. But here's hoping my agent can work a miracle.'

When Tom didn't respond she picked up The Big Blue and shoved it into his arms before he could demur.

'You may as well take this big guy now,' she said. She

wasn't all that sure she could give it to Tom tomorrow without bursting into tears or falling to her knees and begging him to love her back. She'd never been all that good about goodbyes, preferring instead to hold on for dear life.

'I can't accept that,' Tom insisted, backing away.

'And why not?' she asked, flabbergasted. Oh, God, if he was going to ask for the money instead she was stuffed. She'd pretty much spent it all.

'Because it's too personal,' he said.

Personal? Too *personal*? Maggie felt steam rising up her neck. Tom knew more about her, about her feelings and her fears and her failures than even the Wednesday girls did, and he thought her giving him a stupid painting was too personal?

'You painted a picture of yourself for a reason, Maggie. Perhaps you ought to keep it.'

'Every painting I have ever sold has been a painting of somebody, Tom,' she explained. 'That's my schtick. Many of Rembrandt's paintings were self-portraits. Would you not accept one of *those* as a gift because you didn't know the guy in the picture *personally*?'

Tom paused. 'And you're really selling the rest?'

She nodded.

'Does your agent know what they are really about?'

She shrugged. 'In the end it doesn't matter what was going on in my head when they were painted. Whoever buys those paintings would probably rather not know. What matters is whatever pleasure the buyer gets from hanging them on their wall and imprinting their own stories upon them.'

'But I thought that maybe this series was…special. That night, when you saw your face, when you cried all over my shirt, I thought—'

Oh, for heaven's sake!

'I'm broke, Tom!' Maggie all but shouted.

He flinched. But he had no right to make her feel guilty for selling her work. It was her job. He didn't say a word, just watched her, giving her the dark, silent treatment. She felt like reaching out and grabbing him by his sweaty T-shirt and shaking him until he said something. Anything.

'If I don't sell those paintings, then I can't keep this house,' she explained instead, doing her all to keep her breathing under control as she admitted the scary words out loud. 'It's that simple.'

He seemed to be struggling to believe it, so she gave him the whole story. 'You may not have figured this all out as yet, but I'm somewhat of a famous artist. I've made some money, but only in the last couple of years. And that's when Carl looked elsewhere for someone to need him as he thought I no longer did.'

His cheek clenched but he still remained silent.

'I put down the deposit on Belvedere with my money,' she continued, 'and paid for it out of my funds ever since, refusing to take a cent from Carl in the split. And, considering I haven't sold anything new in close to a year, and considering the property prices out this way, let's just say that I've been going backwards fast.'

Tom's throat worked and even in the growing darkness she thought she saw a fire ignite in his gloomy eyes. He was fighting against something while he stood there glaring at her. She could see it. And some fight was better than none. *Keep fighting*, she willed.

'Will you earn enough to keep Belvedere if these paintings sell?'

Maggie shrugged. 'Who knows? But right now, sitting in this room, looking over all this gorgeous furniture, admiring my wondrous view,' she said, her eyes only for him, 'I'm willing to do whatever it takes. Including for evermore damaging my reputation by letting those odds and sods out into the marketplace with my name on them. So stop glowering at me and wish me luck!'

Do it, she begged silently. *Wish me luck at finding a way to stay. Show me some sign that that's why you are so upset right now, because, despite all your hang-ups and history and determination to remain for evermore unaffected, you want me to stay too.*

'Good luck,' Tom said, hooking The Big Blue under his arm. 'I'll see you tomorrow?'

'I'd like that.'

But the sun had set and his face was in shadow and Maggie had no idea what was going on behind those dark hazel eyes as he turned and walked out her door.

CHAPTER ELEVEN

Not long after Tom had left that Thursday night, Maggie received the envelope she had been waiting for. The reason she had kept her front door open day in and day out. The reason she had a telephone sitting on her work desk at all times.

As Maggie stared down at the registered post letter from her lawyer telling her that she was divorced, for the first time in her entire life she felt as if she was truly on her own. Single. Unattached. Free.

She felt as if she could be as spontaneous as she desired; she could run around the house naked, or stand on her head for a half an hour, or drink leftover pasta sauce from the saucepan while jumping up and down on her new couch and nobody could look at her sideways.

For the first time in her life she could truly do whatever she wanted. And she did. Twenty minutes later she was driving up the long driveway leading to Tom's home.

She would have been there in ten minutes but it had taken her that long to finally find out where he lived. His home address wasn't in the phone book, and his cousin Alex's hardware store was already closed so she couldn't grill him. In the end Sandra had provided. She knew a guy who knew a girl who knew a dude whose dad was good friends with the Campbell cousins.

So what now? What could be at the end of this driveway? A caravan on a windy bluff? Or a neat renovation project on which he'd spent the last few years tinkering at night while the town slept?

Maggie finally trundled out of the long, neatly trimmed brush box cave and what she found took her breath away. Immaculate double tennis courts stretched to her right. To her left, an elegant rectangular room housed an indoor pool and from there a winding covered deck, with brilliant crimson bougainvillea dripping from its roof, led to a magnificent one-storey home nestled within the inviting surroundings of delicate willows and towering ghost gums sprawled on the edge of the cliff.

As she pulled up on a square of pebbled ground at the side of the house and switched off her headlights, the full impact of his home came to light. A ground-level veranda wrapped around the structure, which then led towards the cliff to enclose a huge gazebo with a barbecue and what looked like an outdoor spa. And, barely twenty metres from the back of the house, the ground simply dropped away, leaving an un-impeded view of ocean beyond. She'd thought her tree-shrouded view pretty fabulous. But this? This was paradise. And likely worth triple what she'd paid for hers.

She'd thought Tom was too easygoing to run the rat race. Looking at his beautiful home, she wondered if the truth might be that he'd run the rat race, won, and retired on the spoils. Now the words 'richer than Midas' and 'serial heartbreaker' in Freya's tongue came seeping back into her subconscious. She'd thought Freya had been clutching at straws. But she'd been at least half spot on. Had she in fact been totally spot on?

Her breath sounded heavy and damp in the tight confines of her car. *He's* not *like the others*, she told herself. He's not. The *others* had worn their money like a shell. They'd shown it off in their clothes, their cars, their friendships, their diction, and even the way they held their heads, as though looking down at the rest of the world. All Tom had ever shown off was his smile and his charm and his kindness and his sense of humour.

Feeling slightly mollified, Maggie grabbed the bottle of wine she had bought on the way, and alighted from the car. Discreet motion sensors perceived her and a string of elegant gas lamps lit up, surrounding the house in a golden glow.

Her only pair of high-heeled shoes crunched against the pale pebbles and her legs felt weak. She walked to the front door, which had a sign on it saying 'Gone Fishin'. It made her smile, only if for the fact that the men she had looked up to in the past would have died rather than stick such a thing on their front door. Tom *was* different. *That* was what she liked about him.

She ran a hand over her loosely pinned hair, hitched the thin strap of her sky-blue tank top back on to her shoulder, and knocked.

A shuffle came from behind Tom's front door. Maggie briefly considered running and hiding, but her big black Jeep was sitting right in front of the house.

The chain on the door rattled. Maggie wished she had studied science at school rather than arts and that she had discovered a way to turn back time, but unfortunately her wish didn't come true.

The door bumped once on its hinges. Maggie took a deep breath and tried everything in her power to make herself invisible.

The door slowly opened. And all her doubts dropped away. For there was the Tom she knew and loved, standing before her in a soft grey T-shirt and red tartan cotton boxers that revealed a great pair of legs. His hair was a little mussed, as though he'd partaken in an afternoon nap, and he held a box of takeaway noodles in his hand.

Her breath slid from her lungs, thankful that he hadn't opened the door in a tweed suit and carrying a pipe. Despite the elegant surroundings, he was still the same Tom.

'Maggie,' he said, swallowing down a mouthful of noodles. He put the box around the corner on a hidden table and wiped his hands on his shorts. 'What's up?'

Maggie took a deep breath and waved the bottle of wine and wad of papers in her hand. 'I'm divorced,' she said, her voice thick with fear and anticipation and nervous tension. 'And I want to celebrate.'

She thought she saw a flare of something in his eyes but it might have been a trick of the light, because he was suddenly very still.

Maggie kept waving her bottle of red and divorce papers and feeling more and more like a fool with every passing second. If she'd thought him emotionally unavailable before, surely turning up on his doorstep a free woman would be the last thing to jolt him to his senses.

But then he moved, backing into his house so that a lamp somewhere nearby lit his face and she saw it—the heat, the half-smile, the blatant invitation. He held out an arm without a second thought and she went inside.

Now *this is* unexpected, Tom thought, considering that when he'd left her earlier that day he'd been an utter numb-skull, as Alex's seven-year-old would say.

Tom closed the front door. He watched in silence as she put down the papers and wine on a side table and wandered through his house. Her sharp eyes took in the artwork on the walls, the plump well-fed house plants and the understated elegance that he hadn't been able to walk away from when he'd made the move from his home in the big smoke.

He was still getting used to the idea of Maggie in his house. Divorced. With a bottle of wine and a desire to celebrate. And the first place she had come was straight to him. It seemed he didn't have as much time to sort his head as he'd been hoping. It seemed that he was going to have to come to terms with her one way or another tonight.

He caught sight of his reflection in the far window and realised he was dressed like a couch potato, not like a gentleman with a lady caller. He really ought to grab a pair of jeans. He glanced towards his ajar bedroom door, but it was a good twenty feet away. Too far. She was skittish enough to run the second he gave her the chance. And he wasn't going to let that happen.

Not when she had come to him wearing a strappy top with a deep V back exposing acres of creamy smooth skin. Not when her hair was up in some sort of wavy, messy, precarious design that looked as though all he'd have to do was reach up into those smooth waves, remove the one pin holding it all together and it would all come tumbling down. And not when she wore jeans more fitted than he'd ever seen her in before. Sexy jeans. Curve-hugging jeans. Dressed like that, he wasn't planning on letting her out of his sight.

Maggie stopped at his fireplace, above which resided a familiar blue painting. It was already perfectly down-lit as Tom had simply replaced another painting which he now wished he'd put away rather than leaving out for any stray visitor to stumble upon.

She turned to him, noticeably taken aback. 'You've put it up?'

'The minute I got home,' he confessed.

'In the place of a *Drysdale*?' She glared at the classic

Outback painting by one of Australia's most iconic artists, resting haphazardly against the side of his couch, and then back at The Big Blue again. She looked like a kangaroo caught in his Ute headlights.

He couldn't help but laugh when she took a mental step backwards and asked, 'You *own* a Drysdale?'

'And there's a Nolan in my bedroom,' he said, pretty chuffed he'd finally found an opportunity to use that line.

Her eyes widened a fraction further, first at his words and then at the all too clear intention behind them. Her fine chin darted a centimetre upwards before she seemed to remember that she was the one who'd come to him. With wine. And sexy hair. And divorce papers. Her ensuing smile was wry, but at least it was a smile.

'And if I'm not mistaken,' she said, reaching out to a bust hidden in a poky corner of the room, '*that* statue is a Rodin. A knock-off?'

Tom shook his head.

'But it's practically priceless!' she said, her tone accusatory.

'Not quite,' Tom said. 'I managed to pick it up for quite a reasonable price a few years ago.'

He saw the wheels turning in her head as she calculated the lowest price that could have been. He knew he was bragging, but she was there now, and there was no denying he was loaded. The evidence was all around her. And the chance to see her flustered, and pink-cheeked, and on the back foot was too good to give up.

'It was a gift for my sister,' he admitted. 'Tess was the true art fanatic in the family. So to me it *is* priceless.'

Her eyes softened and she let out a small, sympathetic, 'Oh.'

But, in that moment, Tom knew it wasn't about Tess any more. Alex was right—it once had been. For so long everything in his life had been about his beloved little sister, and the wish that he could have been her miracle.

But this, right here, right now, was about him and the woman before him, and not one other thing. He moved further into the room.

'So while you were in Sydney you worked in renovations,' she said, head down, her work-roughened palms making themselves known to the marble, and the history, and the sadness, and the love associated with the small statue.

'I did.'

'But you weren't a labourer.'

'No. I owned the company. I'm an architect by trade and my company became a very successful company, and before moving here I sold it all for a very healthy price,' he said, answering her next few questions so she didn't have to ask them.

'And this house…' She waved a frantic hand around, taking in the vast open-plan, the slate floors, the industrial kitchen, the unimpeded moonlit view across the bay. 'Did you design this?'

He nodded. 'Every last bit. I considered it my last great flight of fancy before retiring from the game.'

Maggie shook her head, waves of hair trembling about her dainty ears and the vulnerable image created a deep well of heat in the pit of Tom's stomach.

'But Tom, it's breathtaking. If you have it in you to create all this, how could you give it up?'

Tom moved closer, arcing around the lounge to get nearer to her. When she realised what he was doing she moved away, subtly, but enough that he couldn't get any closer, until they were practically circling one another about the room.

'Because it was a game,' he said. 'Landing the biggest, the best, the most ridiculously expensive. The more you run with money, the more it falls your way. And it becomes all too important to keep playing faster, harder, longer until the game becomes your life.'

Her eyes widened and he knew she knew exactly what he meant. She'd known men like that before, men like the man he'd been on the way to becoming before it had all turned to a bitter taste in his mouth.

'And then it's too late, before you realise that the actual important things in your life have fallen by the wayside, while you were busy playing,' he said.

Her eyelids flickered and she tugged her bottom lip into her mouth with her top teeth. His gaze was drawn to her mouth, her overbite, her lips, and it took all of his strength to look back at her eyes as she said, 'I always wondered if men like that could come to their senses and realise they were playing the wrong game all along. It seems some can after all.'

Tom nodded, lengthening his strides. She just looked so damned sexy. Haughty. Smoky-eyed. And in his house. It was an irresistible combination. 'So I moved here to give my life over to something real. Good company, good food and working with the sun on my back.'

She stopped when she reached the tinted double pane windows and turned to look out over his perfectly groomed backyard. She crossed her arms and took in a deep breath.

'I didn't mean to let you think otherwise,' he said, 'but it just never seemed like the right time to bring all this up.' He moved in behind her, all the better to wrap himself in her heavenly scent.

'I understand,' she said, her voice lilting and sounding a little bit sad.

'So why do I get the feeling you're disappointed?'

'Because maybe I am. A little.'

He laughed, his breath ruffling the fine hair at the back of her neck, and he heard her deep intake of breath as she realised how close he was.

'You are one funny woman, Maggie Bryce,' he murmured. 'Most people are pleasantly surprised to discover that I am not quite the beach bum.'

'I liked the bum,' she whispered.

And he knew just what she meant. Tom the handyman was fair game. A larrikin. Fling material. The perfect transition guy. Heck, he'd loved being Tom the handyman for several years as much as she'd wanted him to be that person.

But Tom the billionaire was unknown. Intimidating. Self-aware. And perhaps too much of a throwback to the life she had once known. But this was *not* the moment he wanted her pulling away from him.

'Seeing you driving through town in your bandanna and dirty jeans, nobody would think you are one of this country's pre-eminent fine artists, Maggie.'

She let her breath go. 'I know. But I just thought—'

She turned, looked him dead in the eye, and he saw exactly what she thought. She'd thought he might be an uncomplicated way to blot out old hurts. But being here, seeing another side to his personality, meant that he was becoming more real to her by the second.

Well, that was just too bad, for she was already real to him.

He'd seen through her cool shield to the warm heart beneath. He'd seen the way she struggled over her painting because she so wanted to give pleasure to whomever ended up with it hanging proudly in their living room. He'd seen the way she so wanted to be strong and independent when really she had no idea how strong she already was.

And he'd seen his own desire reflected in her eyes. For days. Forbidden desire. But now there was nothing holding them back. So, before she had the chance to think all that natural desire away, Tom took her cheeks in his hands, leaned in and kissed her.

With a soft, resigned sigh and a delicious shiver that Tom felt rumble through her limbs and then his, she shifted in his arms, her long, lean form soft and round against him, as she kissed him right on back.

She threaded her hands through his hair, achingly slowly, pulling him closer still. And Tom couldn't even hope to suppress his groan.

He reached around her waist, taking his time, relishing every touch, every inch of her until his hands found her bare back. She was warm, so very warm. Her skin so soft. He ran his fingers along the bumps of her ribs until they met in the middle and then he simply gave in to his deeper needs and wrapped so tight around her she could have no doubt of how much he wanted her.

Her kiss was so giving. And so trusting. It was instinctive, hot and addictive. The more he had of her, the more he wanted of her. She tasted so sweet. She smelled so sexy. She felt so hot. Tom found himself fast losing his mind.

Finally they came up for air. How long they'd been intertwined he had no idea. All he knew was that he was enamoured. He was taken in. He was completely attached to this woman. If he'd thought himself exposed earlier, open and raw and asking for a world of hurt, he'd had no idea. In that moment he was hers to do with as she pleased.

'Tom,' she murmured, her voice weak, her eyes still closed.

'Yes, Maggie?' he said, pulling away just enough so that he could see her face, her lovely, sweet, delicate face.

Her eyes flickered open, full of shock and wonder. And his heart threatened to burst from his chest.

'What can I do for you, my sweet?' he asked.

But, instead of saying anything, she moved on to her tiptoes and kissed him once, softly, gently, endearingly.

When she pulled away, Tom ran a hand over her cheek, revelling in her soft, warm skin. 'Maggie, you should know that I have wanted this since before I even laid eyes on you.'

Her brow furrowed ever so slightly and Tom leaned down to kiss the creases of worry away. 'Since that first morning when I walked into your house to be greeted with a most unladylike barrage of language.'

A blush crept up her cheeks. 'You heard that?'

'And plenty more since. I've never heard anyone swear in such a sexy manner.' He kissed the tip of her nose. Her cool patrician nose.

'I want you too, Tom,' she said, her voice ragged and wavering. 'I've wanted you since that first day, since you walked into my house with your tool belt and pink pillowcase. Since that first smile that made my toes curl.'

She reached up and ran a soft finger over his lips, her eyes dark and languorous and deep with desire.

That was all the consent Tom needed.

He reached down and scooped her up in his arms. She cradled her head against his chest, snuggling closer, her soft hair tickling at his chin, her warm breath creating goose-bumps along his neck, and he found he wasn't even all that worried that she might hear how loud his heart beat for her.

He walked her across the lounge room and into his huge master bedroom. He'd always loved the size of that room, all that dark wood and coffee-coloured linen, the earthy colours of the simplistic yet brilliant Nolan on the wall contradicting the cool feel of the abundant garden outside his ceiling-to-floor windows. But right now he wished he'd designed it with the bed a heck of a lot closer to the door.

Finally he reached the bed and he let her slide from his arms and to the floor. Slowly, gently, with reverence.

She blinked up at him, her hands resting gently on his shoulders. Ready, but shy. Nervous.

Hell, *he* felt as if this was his first time. With this beautiful, graceful woman for whom he had such strong, confusing, conflicting feelings, all but beckoning him with her dazzling eyes, he suddenly felt all thumbs, with two left feet and no experience.

He stood there and just stared, not having a clue as to what to do next.

And then Maggie, her eyes on his the whole time, let go of him, undid the ribbon at her lower back and, one strap at a time, pulled her dainty top off her shoulders until it fell into a tiny heap at her toes. Her neat long toes with their tiny splatters of blue paint.

When he looked up she was smiling at him, tendrils of her hair curling on to her creamy naked skin, and his nerves fled. A week ago he'd wanted this more than he remembered wanting anything else in his life. But she hadn't been his for the wanting. And now…

Now she was here, unwrapping herself like a precious gift, smiling at him, wanting him right back, and in the end he knew exactly what to do.

Maggie woke up with the delicious scent of cooking calamari tickling at the back of her nose. She breathed in deep and stretched her arms over her head, the fresh cotton sheets feeling sensual as all get out against her naked skin.

Naked skin? She always slept in a tank top and underpants.

Her eyes flew open and it took a few seconds to remember where she was. Her all white bedroom with its peeling wallpaper had been replaced with a cavernous dark room lit only by the discreet golden glow of a lamp in the far corner.

She slid up on to her elbow, dragging the sheet with her, to find she was alone, but there was a perfect Tom-sized indent on the feather pillow beside her.

She reached out and stroked a gentle hand over the indent. She breathed in deeper and, over the scent of calamari cooking somewhere in this huge house of his, she found the scent of Tom. Hot aftershave, hot coffee and hot sunshine.

She lay back against her own pillow with a thud. Letting her arms land in a sprawl above her head, she stretched until she was taking up the whole huge bed, and a grin spread across her face as she admitted that every bit of the dull ache she felt in almost every muscle in her body felt so very, very good.

She tipped her head sideways to find the open door of an *en suite* bathroom. Then, after a quick glance at the bedroom door, she slipped out of bed and made a nudie run for the shower.

Maggie luxuriated under the hot, hard shower spray, reliving the past hours spent in Tom's arms, kissing Tom's skin, drowning in bliss as Tom kissed hers. She tasted salt and realised that she was crying, her tears getting mixed up with the beads of shower water. But she was almost certain it had nothing to do with second thoughts, it was just an overflow of emotion. Necessary tension release. It had been a long time coming.

Meeting Tom, being attracted to Tom, falling for Tom, pulling away, as, no matter how much of a mess Carl had made of their marriage, she'd still had no intention of adding to the horrors by having an affair.

And now she was free! Free to live how she saw fit. And the first thing she had done with this new found freedom was to run straight into another man's arms.

The soap slid unchecked from Maggie's hands.

She tipped the showerhead away, leaving her body cold in the night air. She picked up the soap, Tom's soap, and put it carefully back on to its tray where it belonged.

She cleaned the suds from her suddenly shaking hands, turned off the water and stepped out on to the fluffy white bath mat.

What were you thinking? she asked her foggy reflection in the mirror as she rubbed the thick cotton towel up and down her cool arms vigorously.

I was thinking I wanted those beautiful hands all over my body. I was thinking I wanted to taste those strong lips and run my fingers through that glorious hair and know the look in those burning hazel eyes when they looked at me with devotion and tenderness. That's what I was thinking.

But you couldn't have waited a couple of days? Enough time to see if you were actually going to be living in Portsea for longer than a week?

Well, no, because that might have given me the perfect excuse not to be with him. And I needed to be with him. Just once, to appease the need and want and desire and love that was fast becoming all I thought about any more.

But you know he doesn't yet love himself near enough to be able to truly love anybody else. So you've only set yourself up for heartache.

'Right,' Maggie said out loud. 'Well, this time at least I know that. This time I have come into this forewarned. And forewarned is…what's the saying? Oh, bugger it.'

She pulled a frustrated face at her reflection and stormed into the bedroom to get dressed. After changing back into her tank top and jeans, Maggie took a deep breath and felt as if she was walking the plank to her doom as she followed the scent of seafood to find Tom in his open-plan kitchen.

His hair was damp from a recent shower and he wore low slung jeans and the soft grey T-shirt he'd worn when opening his door earlier that night. Michelangelo's David had nothing on him. This guy made her heart thump so hard in her chest just looking upon him she thought she might faint.

'Hi,' Tom said, smiling at her from the stove on his island kitchen bench.

'Hi,' she said back, suddenly feeling desperately shy.

Well, it had been some time since she had done this. She'd been married for nearly ten years. Though, like every woman of her generation she had seen every episode of *Sex and the City*, she still wasn't quite sure what the protocol was when dealing with the aftermath.

After whispering words of affection in a man's ear before biting down on it so hard it made him cry out. After running her palms over his naked rear end and giving her expert opinion on its beautiful form. After falling asleep in the embrace of a man with whom she had fallen crazy in love, and waking to wonder if she had just made a huge mistake. What was a girl to do?

An antique clock on his mantel chimed ten at night.

'Are you hungry?' Tom asked, licking something off his finger and creating another flashback to the most beautiful, tender, sexy act of lovemaking she had ever experienced.

'Starving,' she said, her voice husky.

Tom smiled with his finger still clamped between his teeth and Maggie suddenly realised she was starving. After having done more physical work in the past two hours than she had in months she was ravenous.

'So, sit,' he said, waving a spatula at a couple of bar stools on the other side of the island bench.

Not knowing what else to do, she did as she was told.

'I caught them myself, last night down at the Rye Pier.'

'Seriously?'

He raised one sexy eyebrow, as though no one had questioned his hunting and gathering ability before.

'I mean I'd never really thought about how one catches calamari before. Maybe on one of those big fishing trawlers out in the middle of the ocean. And I should really shut up now as I am sounding like such a city slicker.'

'Nah,' he drawled, 'I would never *say* such a thing.'

'But you think it,' she said, pointing an accusatory finger his way.

'Every single day,' he admitted and, though it was meant to be an insult, it felt so very much like an endearment.

He grinned at her, all sexy eyes and cheek creases, and her heart thumped against her chest. *Careful*, she thought, sitting straighter to give her heart more room to move.

Should she act as if this was nothing new and thank him for a great roll in the hay and leave?

Should she be polite and sleep over? Or would he panic and think she was clingy?

What would she think of all of this when morning came? Nothing ever looked good at sunrise. Bathed in fresh light, everything always seemed sharper, clearer, wrinklier.

Maggie shifted on her seat. He was watching her. Smiling. He was happy she was still there. He was cooking for her. So she would stay. Until the precise right moment came to leave. Argh!

Tom switched off the stove and walked around the island with the handle of the frying pan in his hand. He sat down next to her, his thigh sliding against hers, and he left it there. His hair was sexily mussed, his T-shirt creased from its time on the floor of his bedroom, and his eyes...his eyes were filled with nothing but her.

She knew then that he wanted her again. More. She knew it deep in her bones. This man. This handyman. This restoration artist. This expert at bringing new life to broken dreams. This hot to trot, sexy, gorgeous, kind, generous man wanted her.

And she knew that she'd come to him that night, not just because she had wanted to make love to him. She'd come to Tom because she was in love with him.

But now that she'd gone ahead and given him what he wanted would that be it? Was she so very easy to leave that after tonight everything would fade? It had happened before. And not only to her, but by him.

After his sister had died, he'd left his business in the middle of the night. Had left behind employees and business partners and people who depended on him. When the going got tough. How was that any different from Carl turning to the calm, easy arms of his law partner when things had become difficult for him at home? Didn't it take a stronger man to face the bad times head on? To talk them through? To do whatever it took to make everything better?

Oblivious to the battle raging in her mind, Tom picked up a piece of calamari in his fingers, blew on it for a few seconds and held it up to her mouth. Weak-willed and enchanted, Maggie opened her mouth and let it inside. The taste exploded on her tongue, the tangy lemon and searing from the pan adding a biting flavour to the morsel.

'That is the most delicious thing in the history of food,' she groaned with her mouth still full.

'Prove it,' Tom said, leaning in to kiss her.

Somehow they ate the whole frying pan full of calamari and finished off the bottle of wine she had brought and, though she was sure it must have all tasted fantastic, Maggie didn't remember another mouthful.

All she remembered later that night as she drifted off to sleep in Tom's arms was the feeling of intimacy and warmth and that look in his eyes. The look that told her that he wasn't going anywhere, and the reckless wish that she could believe him.

As Maggie drifted into the best night's sleep she'd had in six long months, she let the words *I love you* roll about in her mind, as if they were drifting on a surging sea.

CHAPTER TWELVE

TOM woke up early and slowly the next morning, caught halfway between a delicious dream and even more mouthwatering memories of the past twelve hours.

He and Maggie had made love again during the night. They'd taken their time. They'd taken their turn. And as Maggie lay falling asleep in his bed he'd never felt so contented in his whole life.

Tom usually slept with one arm tucked beneath his pillow, the other arm atop the covers and one leg draped over the side of the bed, ready to bolt out the door at a moment's notice if anyone needed him. But that morning he woke curled into a ball, warm, secure, with his arms wrapped tight around...

A pillow. He squeezed. Yep, definitely a pillow. His eyes shot open and he found himself alone in his big bed.

He'd woken up alone in his bed every morning of his life. Even when he'd dated, he'd never had a woman over to his place to stay. Ever. First he'd wanted to keep any stress out of Tess's life and when he'd moved to Sorrento he'd simply wanted to keep stress out of his own life. But that morning as he woke up alone he felt it.

He raised himself up on to his elbow and looked out his bedroom doorway and into his huge house beyond. But he hadn't really been expecting to see Maggie perched on his barstool reading the newspaper.

She was gone. The morning had come and, even after all he had given her, all he'd said and done and felt and witnessed, she'd still left. Because that was what she'd been brought up to do.

He could still smell her perfume on his pillow. If he tried hard enough he could still feel her soft skin beneath his roving hands and the taste of lemon and calamari on her lips. But it wasn't enough. It would never be enough again.

He knew without a doubt that she had left him in a bout of self-protection. She'd left before he'd had the chance to do it to her. Well, if Tom was half the man he hoped he was, if he was worth the trust she had put in him up until that morning, then he was going to damn well run after her.

He pulled himself out of bed and, with a fierce determination lighting his way, he took the fastest shower of his life. For, though she had proven herself quick on her feet, he knew he was quicker.

Especially since he now had that soft sweet voice whispering *I love you* to him just before he fell asleep as the new soundtrack to his life.

Maggie sat on the edge of her own bed staring at a birds' nest in the tree outside her window. A mother bird flew in and three little baby birds popped out their heads, waiting for a feed. Summer had arrived, Maggie realised. When and how had that happened?

Was it really six months ago, at the dawn of winter that she had packed a suitcase and taken the car and the dog and walked away from her city apartment, her work, her so-called friends, her so-called life...

It felt like only yesterday that she had opened her one

suitcase to find she had packed enough underwear for three people, but no toiletries. She had packed a thousand T-shirts, jeans galore and a sequinned gown which she would never have need for out here, but no shoes.

She remembered collapsing to the floor, in the middle of that great front room, and staring out the window at the huge wall of dark forbidding brush while Smiley sat at her side, nudging her to make sure she was okay.

And now she had a bed, a stereo, a view to die for, a complicated man with whom she had fallen in love, and a new letter from the bank telling her to pay up by the end of that weekend or her mortgage would be foreclosed.

She looked up from the letter to see the piece of flaky wallpaper that had been calling to her the whole time she'd lived there. She reached out and grabbed it with both hands and pulled hard enough for a whole strip to come flopping to the ground, leaving old glue and exposed grey plasterboard beneath. But at least the whole house hadn't fallen down around her ears. That was something.

'Nice,' she muttered. 'Feel better now?'

'Maggie?' a familiar voice called out from below.

Her heart rate doubled and she swore under her breath. She really would have to start locking that front door. All of a sudden Belvedere was Grand Central Station and she couldn't keep people away.

Maggie stood, haphazardly redid her ponytail and jogged down the stairs to put on a brave, mature, easygoing face for Tom.

Only to meet him already halfway up the stairs.

'Whoa,' she called out, her hands grabbing at his T-shirt to stop herself from tripping backwards and to stop him from barrelling into her.

'Maggie,' he said, his hazel eyes flashing and beautiful

and brimming with so much energy Maggie could scarcely draw breath.

'Tom,' she whispered, clinging tighter still to the soft cotton, while she told herself that she would one day get over him. One day be able to erase the beauty from the night in his arms from her mind. One day far far away…

'You left,' he accused.

'I did. I thought it best. You didn't owe me breakfast after last night, Tom. Truly. It's okay. I'm okay. We're okay. I just didn't want you to get the wrong idea that I might think that—'

'Who says I'm okay with you leaving in the middle of the night?'

'Well, I just thought that—'

'Well, you thought wrong.'

'Oh,' Maggie said, struggling to keep up with what he was trying to tell her. She unwrapped her fingers from his T-shirt and ran a quick hand over the bunches and creases she'd made. She felt his muscles contract and tighten beneath her accidental caress and his fierce physical response to her gentle touch gave her just enough confidence to ask, 'You *wanted* me to stay?'

'Of course I did. Maggie, I…' He ran a hand over his face and through his hair as she continued straightening his T-shirt. She didn't quite know what she was doing; she only knew she couldn't help herself.

He finally reached down and took her hands in both of his, willing her to look up into his eyes instead. His wounded eyes. Wounded, but determined.

'Maggie, when you came to my door last night, I thought I was dreaming. When I found out that your divorce had come through, I felt like I'd won the lotto. And when I realised I was the first person you had come to see to share the news…'

He stopped, took a deep breath, and if Maggie's hands had been free they would have shaken him to get the words out quicker.

'You what?' You *what*? *You what?*

'Maggie, do you really have no idea how happy that made me? Did nothing we did together last night make it through that tough shield you are trying so hard to assemble around your heart?'

Tom rested her hand against her chest with his above hers. She wished she could slip her hand away so that he could see that, despite the skin and bone and flesh in between his hand and her heart, he was touching it still.

But no. She couldn't. It was better that they not drag this out and get closer and he discover how much she adored him, for when it all turned to crap, as it inevitably would, she just knew that she would never be able to piece herself together again. Not this time. Not after knowing this man. And, though she might have to move if she couldn't get the funds together to keep her home, she was done running. Done hiding.

'Tom,' she said, her voice a little stronger, 'I wasn't kidding yesterday when I told you I'm broke. I'm in big financial trouble and unless Nina can do something magical with those terrible paintings of mine I'm going to have to sell up and move somewhere cheap and cheerful. And away from here.'

And away from you, she thought, but she couldn't say the words for fear she might choke on them.

Tom curled his hand around her fingers, brushing lightly against her breast, before pulling her hands over to his heart. He took a slow deep breath, seeming to pull strength from every fibre of his being. Then he said, 'I know you won't take my money—'

Maggie shook her head vehemently. 'Oh, God, you can't think that I was ever trying to—'

'So I'm not even going to offer it,' he continued. 'But I did get in touch with your agent just now and asked her how much the Blue Smudge Series would be worth on the open market. And, though I think she's a shark and she saw me coming from a mile away and she sounded quite breathlessly ecstatic to get rid of them before anyone else had seen them, I paid what she asked for. And I would think that will keep you with this crazy roof over your head for another good year at least.'

Maggie opened her mouth again to protest, but as though he'd known she would, he leant in and silenced her with a kiss. A soft kiss. A tender kiss. A kiss that took her breath away.

'Don't think of this as some sort of favour,' he said, pulling away at his leisure, his voice now half the volume it had been earlier. And now he was smiling and his hand was stroking her messy hair from her cheek. And Maggie found she was leaning her hips into him. When had that happened?

'I told you from the beginning I liked your blue period,' he said. 'So I bought them. You've seen my place; they match perfectly don't you think?'

Maggie thought. Ridiculous as it seemed, with all that coffee and cream throughout Tom's beautiful home, her Blue Smudge Series would match perfectly, as if she'd been commissioned to paint them specifically for his home. Such a collection of colours could have been borne of the streets of Sorrento with its cream sandy beaches, brown craggy cliffs and clear blue waters.

'But I'm only just divorced,' she said, searching again for the reasons why she knew *she* had to pull back first and not get in too deep and not believe that she could possibly have found love the first time in her life she hadn't gone looking for it.

'Good news,' he said. 'That means you are single. Available. Well, you were for about five minutes. But now if another guy even looks at you sideways he has me to deal with.'

'He does?'

'He does.'

Tom was still stroking her cheek and it felt so nice, so soothing. 'Tom, you can't be somebody's rebound relationship. You're better than that.'

'You bet your sweet patooty I'm better than that, Ms Bryce. Which is why I have every intention of treating you so well you'll never want to leave again.'

Oh, he always knew just the right words to say, this eloquent charmer. He was tempting. So tempting. And temptation had infamously led stronger people than her down the wrong path before. 'But what if—?'

'What ifs are absolutely going to occur, and often,' he said, cutting her off. 'I may disappoint you every now and then. You may drive me up the wall. In fact, I'm kind of looking forward to that part. But Maggie, all that'll just be a sideshow to the main event.'

'The main event?'

He looked so deep into her eyes, she swore in that moment she could see a tunnel all the way to his soul. And it was beautiful.

'The sideshow will pass you right on by, Maggie, for I swear you'll be too caught up basking in the knowledge that I will always love and adore you.'

That was just one thing too much. After their marathon lovemaking session of the night before and being cooped up in her stuffy, skinny, low ceiling staircase for too long, Maggie felt her knees give way. She landed on the midway step with a thud so hard it would leave a bruise.

Tom eased down to sit on the step below. 'Are you okay?' he asked, his voice so full of concern she wanted to cry. Or laugh. Or throw a party.

'Do you realise you just said that you love me?'

Tom smiled. That beautiful, mellow, beguiling smile that came so effortlessly to him and did such strenuous things to her. 'That I did.'

Wow. This was really happening. And now it was her turn to say it. To admit the ridiculous, fantastical truth that she had fallen in love with him right back. She loved him. She loved him. She loved him! She'd admitted it to the girls, she'd admitted it to herself, now all she had to do was admit it to him. Pity the great lug stole her thunder.

'Now I know you love me too,' he said, 'so that's not the issue here. The issue is getting you to stop being so stubborn and realising that you can be with someone in every sense of the word and that disappointment will be part of the deal and that's okay.'

'How do you know that I love you?' she blurted out.

'You told me last night just before you fell asleep in my arms. And snored.'

'I don't snore!'

He'd heard her private whispers? Oh, God. Oh, thank God! The strength returned to Maggie's knees like a rogue wave and she was up and on his lap before he knew what was coming. She wrapped her arms about his neck and held on tight.

'Something you wanted to say, Maggie?' he asked, and Maggie had to hold back from kissing that sexy crease in his right cheek. It sure seemed as if there was going to be plenty of time for all that later.

'I don't really snore, do I?'

'Nah,' he said, grinning. 'You sleep like an angel.'

And she had. Apart from the times he'd woken her to kiss her and ravage her and worship her body, she'd slept and slept and slept. Ocean sounds, schmocean sounds. All it had taken was for her to be in this man's arms. Safe. Protected. Loved.

Maggie shuffled until she was in a more comfy position; she looked him dead in the eye and she let the emotion roiling inside her settle and focus.

Then she said, 'I love you, Tom Campbell. I love your smile and your heart and your goodness and your taste in art and your taste in women. Especially your taste in women. You, my big sweet guy, are *my* lifelong dream. A dream I never really thought would come true.'

'Can I kiss you now?' he asked, wrapping his arms around her too.

'You can,' she said. And he did. Like there was no tomorrow.

'Maybe now you'd like to show me around the rest of your house,' he said huskily a few minutes later.

'No way. Not after seeing your place and discovering you're a bona fide restorer. You'll have a fainting fit when you see the state of the wallpaper in my bedroom.'

'Why don't you show me your bedroom anyway?' he asked, lifting himself and her off the step and slowly sneaking upstairs. 'I promise I won't say a thing about the wallpaper.'

An hour later Tom brought Maggie coffee in bed.

He sat on the edge of her bed, his weight rolling her towards him. 'Your daily bread, madam.'

She sat up, took the drink and had a great sip. It was bitter, hot and delicious. 'Perfect,' she said, smiling up at him.

'So are you going to loll about in bed all day, or are we going to take that walk down to your little beach as promised?'

'The beach!' Maggie shoved her coffee into Tom's hands

and leapt out of bed, dressing again in super-quick time. 'I'd totally forgotten about the beach! What are we waiting for?'

'Right,' Tom said, leaving the coffee on her bedside table. 'I see where I'm going to come in the grand scheme of things. Coffee. Beach—'

'Smiley!' Maggie called out. 'We're going for a walk!'

'Smiley, then me,' Tom grumbled. As she bounced about the room, pulling on her jeans two legs at a time, she saw Tom staring at the huge strip of wallpaper which had been torn from the wall.

'Unless of course you want to ditch this white elephant once and for all and move in with me.'

Maggie stopped bouncing. 'We can't sell Belvedere. They'll knock it down for sure.'

The look in Tom's eyes showed that even he, the great renovator, seemed to think that might be for the best. She poked out her bottom lip and whimpered for all she was worth.

'Fine,' he finally said, sighing dramatically. 'We can live here and keep my place as a weekender. I'm sure there are a thousand other jobs we can find for me to do on this place to keep me out of trouble.'

Live here? He wanted to live here? With her and Smiley and the paint fumes and…

Maggie was in his arms again, slamming him back on to the bed before she could even finish that thought.

Another hour later, they walked across the lumpy backyard with its weed-infested rocky ground.

'I love what you've done with the place,' Maggie said. It really was amazing. Where the brambles had once been king there was now naught but open air.

Together they traversed the haphazard path made out of flat

rocks implanted into the already rocky slope, Tom going first and holding Maggie's hand the whole time. He stopped every now and then to take her around the waist to make sure she didn't slip, though she was fairly sure he was copping a feel half the time.

She told him so, and he only let his hands slip higher. And she didn't mind in the least.

When they reached the bottom and Maggie was standing on the edge of the tiny beach, which would have been five metres at its deepest and perhaps fifteen metres wide, she felt…fabulous.

She felt even better than she had imagined it would make her feel. Though she had a feeling that feeling had a little to do with the man there with her, holding her hand.

'You first,' he said.

'Together,' she insisted. 'On three. One, two—'

But, as well as having no skills with a chainsaw, Smiley also couldn't count. He scooted past them with all the dexterity of a mountain goat and lolloped along the virgin sands, leaving a jagged row of doggy footprints.

They both laughed. 'So much for the grand reopening of your beach,' Tom said.

'Story of my life,' she said. 'Never expect anything to go according to plan.'

'Mmm,' Tom said, turning her and drawing her back into his arms and lifting her and carrying her on to the beach. 'I'm beginning to see that about you. Even so, I think you really should plan to stay,' Tom said, his voice deep and low and insistent and concerned and sexy as hell. 'For ever.'

'For ever,' Maggie repeated, and for the first time in her whole life she could see for ever stretching before her, years and years of eating The Sorrento Sea Captain's beer-battered fish, and walking these sands, and holding this hand. And it made her smile, a big toothy grin that made her cheeks hurt.

'Only if you do too,' she said.

And, as he lowered his smiling mouth to hers, Tom promised, 'Count on it.'

* * * * *

THE ROYAL HOUSE OF NIROLI
Always passionate, always proud
The richest royal family in the world—
united by blood and passion,
torn apart by deceit and desire

Nestled in the azure blue of the Mediterranean Sea, the majestic island of Niroli has prospered for centuries. The Fierezza men have worn the crown with passion and pride since ancient times. But now, as the king's health declines, and his two sons have been tragically killed, the crown is in jeopardy.

The clock is ticking—a new heir must be found before the king is forced to abdicate. By royal decree the internationally scattered members of the Fierezza family are summoned to claim their destiny. But any person who takes the throne must do so according to The Rules of the Royal House of Niroli. Soon secrets and rivalries emerge as the descendents of this ancient royal line vie for position and power. Only a true Fierezza can become ruler—a person dedicated to their country, their people…and their eternal love!

Each month starting in July 2007,
Harlequin Presents is delighted to bring you
an exciting installment from
THE ROYAL HOUSE OF NIROLI,
in which you can follow the epic search
for the true Nirolian king.
Eight heirs, eight romances, eight fantastic stories!

Here's your chance to enjoy a sneak preview of the first book delivered to you by royal decree…

FIVE minutes later she was standing immobile in front of the study's window, her original purpose of coming in forgotten, as she stared in shocked horror at the envelope she was holding. Waves of heat followed by icy chill surged through her body. She could hardly see the address now through her blurred vision, but the crest on its left-hand front corner stood out, its *royal* crest, followed by the address: *HRH Prince Marco of Niroli...*

She didn't hear Marco's key in the apartment door, she didn't even hear him calling out her name. Her shock was so great that nothing could penetrate it. It encased her in a kind of bubble, which only concentrated the torment of what she was suffering and branded it on her brain so that it could never be forgotten. It was only finally pierced by the sudden opening of the study door as Marco walked in.

"Welcome home, *Your Highness*. I suppose I ought to curtsy." She waited, praying that he would laugh and tell her that she had got it all wrong, that the envelope she was holding, addressing him as Prince Marco of Niroli, was some silly mistake. But like a tiny candle flame shivering vulnerably in the dark, her hope trembled fearfully. And then the look in

Marco's eyes extinguished it as cruelly as a hand placed callously over a dying person's face to stem their last breath.

"Give that to me," he demanded, taking the envelope from her.

"It's too late, Marco," Emily told him brokenly. "I know the truth now...." She dug her teeth in her lower lip to try to force back her own pain.

"You had no right to go through my desk," Marco shot back at her furiously, full of loathing at being caught off-guard and forced into a position in which he was in the wrong, making him determined to find something he could accuse Emily of. "I trusted you...."

Emily could hardly believe what she was hearing. "No, you didn't trust me, Marco, and you didn't trust me because you knew that I couldn't trust you. And you knew that because you're a liar, and liars don't trust people because they know that they themselves cannot be trusted." She not only felt sick, she also felt as though she could hardly breathe. "You are Prince Marco of Niroli.... How could you not tell me who you are and still live with me as intimately as we have lived together?" she demanded brokenly.

"Stop being so ridiculously dramatic," Marco demanded fiercely. "You are making too much of the situation."

"*Too much?*" Emily almost screamed the words at him. "When were you going to tell me, Marco? Perhaps you just planned to walk away without telling me anything? After all, what do my feelings matter to you?"

"Of course they matter." Marco stopped her sharply. "And it was in part to protect them, and you, that I decided not to inform you when my grandfather first announced that he intended to step down from the throne and hand it on to me."

"To protect me?" Emily nearly choked on her fury. "Hand

on the throne? No wonder you told me when you first took me to bed that all you wanted was sex. You *knew* that was the only kind of relationship there could ever be between us! You *knew* that one day you would be Niroli's king. No doubt you are expected to marry a princess. Is she picked out for you already, your *royal* bride?"

* * * * *

*Look for THE FUTURE KING'S PREGNANT MISTRESS
by Penny Jordan in July 2007,
from Harlequin Presents,
available wherever books are sold.*

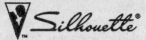

Silhouette®
Romantic
SUSPENSE

**Sparked by Danger,
Fueled by Passion.**

Mission: Impassioned

A brand-new miniseries begins with

My Spy

By *USA TODAY* bestselling author

Marie Ferrarella

She had to trust him with her life....
It was the most daring mission of Joshua Lazlo's
career: rescuing the prime minister of England's
daughter from a gang of cold-blooded kidnappers.
But nothing prepared the shadowy secret agent
for a fiery woman whose touch ignited something
far more dangerous.

My Spy

#1472

Available July 2007 wherever you buy books!